IN SEARCH of a NAME

IN SEARCH
of a NAME

a novel

Marjolijn van Heemstra

TRANSLATED BY JONATHAN REEDER

ATRIA BOOKS

NEW YORK   LONDON   TORONTO   SYDNEY   NEW DELHI

ATRIA
BOOKS

An Imprint of Simon & Schuster, Inc.
1230 Avenue of the Americas
New York, NY 10020

First Atria Books hardcover edition November 2020

ATRIA B O O K S and colophon are trademarks of Simon & Schuster, Inc.

For information about special discounts for bulk purchases, please contact Simon & Schuster Special Sales at 1-866-506-1949 or business@simonandschuster.com.

The Simon & Schuster Speakers Bureau can bring authors to your live event. For more information or to book an event, contact the Simon & Schuster Speakers Bureau at 1-866-248-3049 or visit our website at www.simonspeakers.com.

Interior design by Kyoko Watanabe

Manufactured in the United States of America

1 3 5 7 9 10 8 6 4 2

Library of Congress Cataloging-in-Publication Data has been applied for.

ISBN 978-1-9821-0048-3
ISBN 978-1-9821-0050-6 (ebook)

For Eyse and, of course, David

"In talking about the past we lie with every breath we draw."

WILLIAM MAXWELL,
So Long, See You Tomorrow

IN SEARCH
of a NAME

IF I HADN'T turned eighteen twelve years after a distant uncle in his bungalow in Spain sensed his end was near; if he hadn't been childless and, on his deathbed, nostalgic for what might have been; if he hadn't therefore sent his ring, his only piece of jewelry, to my grandmother with the instructions to bequeath it to a future family namesake; if my grandmother hadn't forgotten to buy me a present for my eighteenth birthday and if I hadn't dropped in on her that day; if she hadn't anxiously glanced around the room for something that even vaguely resembled a present; if her eye had not fallen upon the small black leather box with the ring that had been waiting for twelve years for the right finger; if I hadn't saddled myself with a promise that meant my first pregnancy would be completely dominated by a bomb attack on December 5, 1946, then this story would have remained the tenuous, slippery myth it had been for some seventy years.

"WE'LL NAME HIM Frans," I say. "Frans Julius Johan."

I'm startled by the volume of my voice.

"I'm standing right next to you," D laughs. "You don't have to shout."

He opens the passenger door. "Need a hand?"

"I'm pregnant, not handicapped."

Grinning, he walks around to the driver's side. Before getting in, he raps twice on the roof of the car. Superstition. D thinks that with too much happiness, you have to ward off mishaps. I try to feel relieved. The uncertain weeks have passed: a heart is beating, a child is growing. But alongside the relief, a fear nestles in my chest, the fear that has been skulking around in my body ever since that blue plus sign appeared on the pregnancy test. It is a menacing void that seems to grow along with the baby. Big and blank and white, like the map of Antarctica a friend gave me last year for my birthday. A vast patch with the name of the continent at the upper left, the scale on the lower right, and otherwise nothing. No roads, no lakes, no villages. The friend thought he had found the coolest map ever, but it gave me goose bumps. Ever since we've started counting down the weeks, I can't get that white blotch out of my head, that terrifying combination of something and nothing.

I sink into the seat and clench my teeth at the stabbing pain in my hip. Thirteen weeks pregnant and already pelvic instability. D flops down next to me and points to the folder of photos I'm holding. "Let's have one more look." Together we examine the images the ultrasound technician had printed out for us ("New snapshots of your little one!") after she's clarified the various splotches of light on the screen. An arm, a stomach, a pumping heart: our child manifested in glowing body parts. I nodded dutifully at everything she named, but I could not make out anything human in the shapes drifting in the darkness. They looked more like primitive creatures in the primordial soup. The photos resemble a misty nighttime landscape. D thumbs through them. I know which one he's looking for: the one with the two long blotches—legs—and a small protrusion in between. The photo where the technician exclaimed, "There you are: a son!"

D was relieved. The possibility of a daughter scared him. So vulnerable. I fear just the opposite. Boys, I once read, more frequently die a reckless death—cars, alcohol, war, fireworks, brawls.

"So quiet in here," D mumbles. He puts the key into the ignition and tunes the radio to 10 Gold, his favorite station. When he's found the photo, he traces the contour of the shapes with his finger and hums contentedly along with Elton John. I look at my hands, at the thick gold ring with the blue stone that my grandmother solemnly slid onto my middle finger on my eighteenth birthday, exacting from me the promise that I would name my first-born son after the family hero whose ring it had been. She uttered his name as though she were revealing a secret. *Frans Julius Johan.* It was the first time I had ever heard his real name; I only knew him from the sobriquet the family had given him: *Bommenneef,* "Cousin Bomber." A hero of the Dutch Resistance who, more than a year after the war's end, carried out an attack on a Dutch Blackshirt who had escaped prosecution because he could not live with the idea that justice was found wanting. His last wish, according to my grandmother, was that the ring be worn by a namesake. "That thing's been sitting in the cupboard for twelve years. We could wait for an eternity until this family produces a namesake, but I could also just give it to you with the agreement that you'll name your first son after him."

"We'll name him Frans." That strange, loud voice again. "Frans Julius Johan."

D looks up from the folder, smiling. "Aren't we supposed to spend months agonizing over a name? Let alone *three* first names?"

I shake my head. There's no doubt in my mind. "We're naming him after Bommenneef. The world could use a bit of courage and self-sacrifice these days."

D is taken aback. "Are you serious? I thought that whole

Bommenneef thing, that namesake promise, was more like a . . ." He's searching for the right words. "A juicy story, you know, for parties and all. Not something you really wanted."

He's right. It was that kind of story. The perfect anecdote to contribute to half-drunken debates over lawlessness and retribution, the tale of the hero after whom I would one day name my son. And, to be honest, also just an attempt to impress people with my illustrious family history whenever they noticed that eye-catching ring on my middle finger. For fifteen years it's been a noncommittal topic; Bommenneef always felt as distant and intangible as the child I would name him after. The one no longer existed, the other did not yet exist. All they had in common was the story. But now that the future son has presented himself as an as-yet-unknown reality, I need a legend for my map. A name that will put things into proportion, a story to fill that gaping white hole. And this is just the story I need. A hero as the blueprint for my son.

I look at the ultrasound photos again, and for a moment it's as if Bommenneef is floating there in the darkness. Half swallowed up by history, yearning for light and life. I don't feel like telling D about Antarctica and spoiling today with my fear of the unknown. D starts the car and drives us out of the parking lot.

"It was his last wish," I say.

"But he's been dead for almost thirty years."

"I promised my grandma."

"She's dead too."

"What have you got against it?"

"I can think of nicer names."

"It's the story behind the name that counts."

"But you hardly know anything about him."

I lay our misty landscape on the dashboard.

D is right again. What I know can be summed up in a single sentence: Resistance hero delivers a parcel bomb disguised as a Sinterklaas present to an ex-Nazi.*

I write "bomb," but according to the family narrative, the bomb was always a "little bomb," the Blackshirt was a "rat," and Bommenneef "a rascal." It was my grandparents' generation that kept the tale alive, repeating it every chance they got, to whoever would listen. Rascal startles rat with bomblet.

A tale full of diminutives, to which my grandmother attached two more diminutives: *loontje* and *boontje*.

She was the one who first told me about Bommenneef. I was seven. We were in The Hague, on the way to a cocktail party at one of her hundreds of friends or shopping at the Bonneterie, I can't really remember. I was the only of her ten grandchildren she took with her on such outings. Probably because I was the kind of child who could entertain herself for an hour with paper and colored pencils under a table, but also because I was named after her. I always noticed how she glowed whenever I introduced myself. "Same as me!" she would cry, as though the existence of a small version of herself were a permanent marvel. I don't know if our passing along the Prinsengracht was a coincidence, or whether she took an intentional detour, but either way we found ourselves standing in front of a brownstone. Grandma pointed to the door where the "little bomb" had been delivered and told me about our family hero. She drew

---

*Sinterklaas, or St. Nicholas Day, is celebrated annually with the giving of gifts on the evening of December 5.

my attention to the color of the façade, a few shades lighter than the neighboring houses. "They had to rebuild the house, you see." She ended her story with a jolly *Boontje komt om zijn loontje*—"Tuppence gets his comeuppance." I had no idea who *Boontje* was, and what kind of *loontje* he came for, but I nodded because it sounded right. Only later did I discover the proverbial power of full rhyme. Haste makes waste. No pain, no gain.

Since then, I have retold the Bommenneef story countless times, and the more I told it, the more detailed it became.

In fifth grade I even presented it in a largely fictitious show-and-tell. The rat in this version had been expanded to a gang of twelve Blackshirts whom my super-uncle blew to smithereens one Sinterklaas evening with his parcel bomb. I had practiced counting down at home in the mirror, my voice pregnant with pent-up tension—four, three, two, one, kaboom!—and then sank to the floor with grand, dramatic gestures—four, three, two, one!—where I played dead until the applause broke out. I got an A+ and a standing ovation from my classmates. An added reward for my direct kinship with a hero of such stature was a monthslong romance with the most popular boy in school. And although the incident was the culmination of coincidences—a birthday, a forgotten present, a death twelve years earlier—becoming the heir to the ring on my eighteenth birthday seemed entirely logical. Historical justice. Full rhyme.

"Well?" D asks as we drive into our neighborhood. He gracefully maneuvers the car through the narrow streets.

Perhaps it's crazy to cling to an old hero, to a simple childhood rhyme. But when D asks which ultrasound photo we should hang on the fridge, I once again feel that vast white void under my navel.

"You're right, I don't know much. But I'm going to find out."

D smiles his big, contagious smile, the smile that got him cast for a Mentos ad that has been showing on prime-time TV for some five years now. *The Freshmaker.* I love that smile, and the carefreeness with which he replies that I'd better get cracking, then.

WHERE DOES A heroic tale begin? With the evil that is eventually defeated? With the deed itself? With the hero? With the courage required to do what needs to be done, putting one-self on the line? And what sparks that courage? Injustice? Fear? The desire to capture that fear, to hold it up to the light, to be able to say, "I am not afraid"?

I start my quest for information about Bommenneef's life by calling the oldest aunt in my family. This one phone call sets off the grapevine of well-to-do seniors who knew Bommenneef, or who know people who knew him. Word of my search travels at lightning speed through retirement-home coffee nooks and golf club canteens.

Every day I receive new snippets of information by phone, email, and old-fashioned post. I decide to make two folders on my computer: "Facts" and "Other." The first one consists of a single document containing no more than a few sentences. Bommenneef—Frans Julius Johan—was born in Haarlem in 1909 and died in 1987. He was my grandfather's second cousin. He had two older sisters, both now deceased; his father was in the army; his mother died young. He worked as a consultant for Staalglas Amsterdam and as a salesman for Citroën. After the war he became head of the motor vehicle facility at the military garrison in The Hague. Almost everything else ends up in the second folder, a colorful miscellany of memories, hearsay, and loose scraps of information.

His sisters' children—his nearest relatives—appear to know the least about him. They only saw Bommenneef infrequently. None of his nephews or nieces can tell me any more about the bombing than I already know. It is with the periphery of the family and vague acquaintances where the most vivid memories endure. As though to really know him required a certain distance.

Someone tells me how Frans swam around his houseboat—with slow strokes, like a lethargic frog; someone says he almost crashed his race car at the 1936 Monaco Grand Prix; someone knows for sure that he was given a life sentence for the bombing and got into a brawl with a cellmate in a Leeuwarden prison who had refused to serve in Dutch East India ("Communist scum," Frans called conscientious objectors); someone knows for sure he got away with the bombing; someone says Queen Juliana pardoned him; someone says he committed suicide in his jail cell; various people claim he ended up in Spain, which, considering the attack was committed on Sinterklaas Eve, I find too silly to take seriously.* A niece of my grandfather's describes Frans as a Casanova, dark and handsome, "the heartbreaker of Haarlem." An uncle says he was short and stocky. No one has any photographs.

I learn that there are various versions of the bomb legend. One good-natured uncle is convinced that the Blackshirt was killed instantly. He soft-pedals: "He was an old man anyway." A scandalmonger aunt tells me that after the explosion, the man lay for hours on the stoop, fighting for his life. Someone says that Frans acted on a government directive, another says that after the attack he never uttered another word. Every version has its own shade and slant, with two uncontested main ingredients: Frans's heroism and the villain's well-deserved death. Why he sent the ring to my grandmother in particular, no one can say. They assume it had to do with her role within the family. My grandmother was the family fixer, someone known to be able to finagle anything. Even an heir.

Details come to light that link his life to mine via the most unexpected places and people.

I also know he frequented Amsterdam cafés, and he regularly walked along the same route I took every day while cycling to classes. He lived one street behind the house where, sixty years later, I rented my first room. A good friend of mine has an atelier in the garrison where Frans started his postwar military career. Now I roam through the hallways where he must have walked; for the first time I study the bland, gray stone walls,

---

*St. Nicholas (Sinterklaas) and his helper Piet are said to come from Spain.

and try to imagine that Frans, too, touched these tiles and trod these floors. I sneak a cigarette (the last one, the very very last one!) through an open window and think back on the slugs on my grandmother's patio. How they slid over the paving stones, across the dirt, the plants, seemingly from nowhere to nowhere, but as soon as the sun broke through, there was suddenly a glistening trail of slime that connected everywhere the snails had been in the course of their sluggish trek.

D and I go to city hall, where he has to acknowledge paternity. It is the same counter where, a few months from now, we'll have to register the baby's name.

D is still skeptical about naming him after Bommenneef. He says there are plenty of other Dutch heroes to choose from. Floris. Willem. Maurits.

"But he's *our* hero," I say.

"*Your* hero. And do you really like that name? Frans?"

"It's not about whether I like it or not. It fits."

D says that a name always fits in the end, that a name is like a leather shoe that forms itself to the foot.

But in my mind, it's the other way around: A person grows into his name. The name is the foot.

"You're making too big a deal of it," D says.

"It *is* a big deal."

He places his hand on my belly. "Four inches is not that big."

"But it's growing. It's growing by the second. Eighteen years from now we'll have six feet of person."

The numbers on the electronic screen jump ahead. It's our turn. The civil servant behind the gleaming counter asks what the child's last name will be. D looks questioningly at me. "Mine, right?" I nod. That's what we had decided. I get the first name, he the last. After D has signed the form, the official congratulates us. "Now the child is officially both of yours."

Back home, we start clearing out the junk room that will become the nursery. D claims veto rights regarding the first name. I disagree. Irked, he asks why we have to name our child *after* anyone at all.

"Because it gives you something to go on. It's a framework, a story you step into."

"So why this story?"

"Because it's a good story, the most reassuring one I have."

I am surprised by my choice of words. Is it really reassuring? As a child, the story of Bommenneef confirmed my sense of justice. Reward and retribution. The certainty that good wins in the end.

"He's not even here yet," D sighs, "and you already want to reassure him."

I nod. "Something like that."

"Or reassure yourself."

"I want a moral compass, a name to navigate with."

"It's a kid, not uncharted territory."

I don't tell him this is exactly how I feel.

D shakes his head, mutters something about hormones, and starts screwing together an antique cradle we picked up last week from an aunt. He calls it the "horror crib" because the combination of the creaking dark wood and the faded pink flowered awning fabric gives him the creeps.

25 WEEKS LEFT

THE BABY IS now about four and a half inches long; mom blogs show avocados and pomegranates as points of reference. They inform me that the ears are now in the right place, and that he is covered in down. My nails grow so fast that I have to clip them every couple of days. Long dark hairs are growing around my navel. Masculine hormones, says the obstetrician. D calls me "werewolf" and pretends to get a fright when I walk into the bedroom at night. Or maybe he's not pretending.

My belly swells up—a week ago I looked like I'd just put on some weight, but now I'm very obviously pregnant. This should be, according to all the books and blogs, the best time of the pregnancy: the second trimester, when the nausea has passed and your belly is not yet gigantic. But every morning it's like I have to hoist myself out of a swamp before I can function normally. My limbs feel bogged down and soggy, as though my blood is more viscous than usual. I cry over the stupidest things—yesterday, over a squashed avocado on the bike path that just lay there, green and soft and defenseless in the rain. Four and a half squashed inches.

Since a few days ago I think I feel the baby move. Going by what the books and websites say, it should be something like "a butterfly painting the inside of your belly" or "gentle tickling under your navel," but this has nothing to do with tickling, it's the rumbling of a volcano: small, restrained explosions and ominous gurgling. Postnatal care has to be arranged, the bed needs leveling, the insurance company notified; there's something absurd about it, all these chores for four and a half inches of person.

When the obstetrician brings up pain management during delivery, I want to tell her that it's all one big misunderstanding, that I'm only pregnant with an idea, that there's really not a person growing inside me. The gurgling below my navel can't possibly be a portent of real-life legs that will one day roam our planet, that will turn left or turn right, follow wrong paths in a huge, messy life. I want to tell her that should something come out of me and into this world, it will be simpler than all that. Something with a heart and maybe some human features, but beyond that a purely temporary presence. Something soft, no more than form and warmth, which will then disappear.

But the only thing that disappears is me. Slowly but surely, I am making way for the baby. A layer of fat is enveloping me, my breasts are being swallowed up by larger breasts, my feet by larger feet.

———————

The slug trail glistens on. An elderly uncle tells me that in the 1930s Frans was in the cigar business and bought his tobacco leaves at an auction house on the Nes.

I ask him which number.

"No idea," he replies, "but they called it 'the Hell of Frascati,' because it was hot and smoky, and the traders were cutthroat when it came to getting their hands on the best leaves."

Frascati! The building that, in the seventies, was renovated into the theater where I now work.

After a performance about the forgotten heroes of the Resistance, I tell a colleague, a woman in her seventies, about my search and this crazy Frascati coincidence. She looks at me, dumbstruck.

"Bomb attack? Sinterklaas Eve?"

I nod.

"You mean the guy who swam across the river with a knife clamped in his jaw?"

"No, or yes, maybe . . . I've never heard anything about that knife part."

"Could be just an urban legend."

"What legend?"

"Did that attack really happen?"

I take her hand, drag her to the theater café, and sit her down. "Tell me what you know."

"There was a boy at school who used to brag about his uncle during recess," she says. "It wasn't his blood uncle, I don't think, but the brother of an aunt by marriage, or something. He told us that during the war, the man swam across a river with a knife in his mouth to pick up some folks who had fled to England,* and when he got to the far side he realized they'd been ratted on, and that after the war, dressed up like St. Nicholas, he murdered the man who betrayed them. On Sinterklaas Eve, with that same knife, and a bishop's miter on his head. Nobody believed him, because the kid was such a braggart. We teased him about it for years. If you want, I can find out where he lives now."

"Yes, please," I say. "That would be great."

The next morning she phones me with the number of a nephew of Elize, Bommenneef's eldest sister.

K receives me a few days later in his small service apartment in Baarn. His father's brother had been married to an Elize. K only met Frans twice—Frans and his sister, he says, didn't really see eye-to-eye. All he remembers about Frans was that he was tall. "But maybe," he corrects himself, "that was only because I was still little."

I ask him about the story of the river and the knife. "We heard that from Elize, once," he says. "The only time I ever heard her talk about her brother. Just a few sentences, and that was it. She got angry when I pressed her for more." He admits making up the part about Bommenneef going to the Prinsen-

---

Engelandvaarders (literally: England-seafarers) were men and women who attempted to escape from the Netherlands across over 100 miles of the North Sea to reach England during World War II. Only about one in ten were successful in the crossing; a large number of them were either killed or arrested en route or died at sea. Of those who did reach England, many joined the Allied forces or served with the Dutch government-in-exile.

gracht dressed up like St. Nicholas. "I figured it was good for the story." All he knows is that it happened, and that Bommenneef went to jail, no more than that.

K has brought out a stack of ancient photo albums and lays them on the coffee table. There's not a single photo of Frans. For nearly an hour he regales me with prewar class pictures and five decades of vacation snapshots. I try to stay patient and focused, albeit with the dwindling hope that anything useful about Frans will emerge.

After we've sifted through all the albums, K serves scalding-hot tea and sets down a dish of After Eights. He fixes his watery gaze on me. "You look like him," he says. "Same eyes, same mouth."

I'm taken aback by his observation. In my fantasy, Frans always has the typical hero looks. Full lips, chiseled jaw, scarred face—not my narrow, unmenacing features. It never occurred to me that the shared gene pool might reveal itself in my own face.

I ask if he can remember how Frans spoke and moved, how he dressed, his expression. K just shakes his head. He has no answers.

If he has nothing to offer, I can just as well leave. I take a gulp of tea, burn my mouth. Another gulp. I really want to get out of here. But K is clearly not planning to let me go. Just before I've drained my teacup, he refills it and launches into a monologue about his life. The more he talks, the less likeable he becomes. He refers to women his age as "sucked-out oysters": dry and gray and stinking of fish. He grumbles that everything that went wrong in his life was because of someone else's stupidity.

When I get up from the sofa and say I mustn't keep him any

longer, he says I haven't seen the most important thing yet. He walks to the cupboard next to the window, takes out a small stack of paper, and places it on the table. "Elize's life story. She typed it herself before she died." Why only bring this up now, I want to ask him, but I realize he probably saved it for last on purpose. I sit back down and, my hope rekindled, slide the sheets toward me.

Seven pages, single-spaced. Elize begins by describing her early youth in the aloof aristocratic circles that I recall having heard about from older generations. High expectations, scant affection, a hermetic world of nannies and a few carefully selected playmates. She describes how in the 1910s she and her younger brother Frans went to school in Zutphen on a donkey cart, how her parents were always busy fulfilling social obligations, leaving the childrearing to English governesses. She writes about playdates with Princess Juliana at Noordeinde Palace, and about a castle belonging to an auntie in Doorn where all the cousins would get together in the summer, until in 1919 they sold it to Wilhelm II, the last German kaiser, who lived there until his death. She goes into great detail about the war, the Hunger Winter, and the years thereafter, when she had to take on all manner of jobs to make ends meet because her husband's business went bankrupt. She writes about her travels, her children, grandchildren, and step-grandchildren, and their vicissitudes. She writes about everything except that fateful Sinterklaas Eve. Not a word about Frans as an adult.

All I've got is that boy on the donkey cart. I picture a narrow, serious face, a sailor's suit, sharply parted hair, an absent expression. A privileged, neglected little boy.

With my eyes and my mouth.

NEWS OF MY quest has spread to the farthest branches of our family tree. A distant aunt calls me to report that her son-in-law, a collector of old books, bought a box full of stuff belonging to Frans at an auction last month. "He walked past it, had no idea what was inside, but saw 'Van Heemstra 1945' on the box, so he took it. And guess what was inside!" She waits. I don't want to guess, I want to know. "No idea. Tell me."

"Bommenneef's pictures and papers!" she exclaims. "I'll be in Amsterdam this week, so I can bring it along. Just give me your address."

Still reeling from her announcement, I stammer out our street name.

The aunt carries on enthusiastically, telling me that the box had been in the attic of a collector of old documents, and that it's probably the contents of Frans's desk drawers. I have so many things to ask her, but don't get any further than shell-shocked mumbling. Frascati, the colleague, now this box. Aunt S says she'll come by the day after tomorrow, then hangs up.

"Creepy," D says when I tell him. "How's this much coincidence possible?"

In fact, I find these implausibilities reassuring. It's as though the history of Bommenneef has attached itself to me like a barnacle, like the story chose me, rather than the other way around. It's sneaking into my life, bit by bit, validating itself, making itself jibe.

Two days later, Aunt S places the cardboard box on our kitchen table. The block letters on the lid are sloppily written but legible enough: Van Heemstra 1945. She carefully removes the lid and shows me the envelopes into which she has separated the contents. Taxes. Insurance. Traffic tickets. Photos. "Just to get you started. It was complete chaos, as if somebody had just dumped the entire contents of the desk drawer into the box all at once. Maybe after his arrest, or when he was in jail. There must have been someone looking after his affairs." But who it was, she doesn't know.

My fingers glide over the envelopes. Deep down I was prepared for this to turn out to be some kind of joke, but the box looks old and battered, and my aunt is just as amazed as I am at the find.

She replaces the lid and says that now I have an obligation to history to fill in the gaps. For the first time, it occurs to me what a nice expression it is: that history is a living presence you can be obliged to.

As soon as she's gone, I lay the contents of the envelopes side by side. I quickly skim the dates on the letters and receipts: they go up until December 1946, just before the bombing.

It's bizarre to see dates that one usually equates with war and concentration camps in run-of-the-mill letters from the city council. Even in October 1944, taxes were paid and traffic tickets issued. I have always associated the occupation of the Netherlands with anarchy and chaos, with dysfunctional institutions. But in November 1941, Frans took out a life insurance policy for *f* 71.30. The box also contains twenty-eight traffic tickets. Apparently, the prewar speed limit was 60 kilometers per hour; Frans often drove 80. There are no speeding tickets during the time of the occupation, but he did park illegally seven times, and once drove the wrong way down a one-way street.

Aunt S is probably right—someone must have emptied out his desk after his arrest, intending to save the contents until Frans was released. The handover apparently never took place. Maybe there was a falling-out, perhaps the keeper of the documents lost contact with Frans during his jail time. I can't imagine that a person would deliberately save inconsequential letters and traffic fines. They were probably simply forgotten; this was one of those boxes that sits at the back of a cupboard for years and gets moved from one address to the other because nobody bothers to look inside. Until one day, when those mundane, everyday things suddenly become historical documents.

Underneath the envelope with traffic fines is a white folder on which my aunt has written "Photos (1911–1946)" with a black felt-tip pen. I hesitate. This will be the first time I see him. I gingerly open the envelope and lay the contents on the table.

On top is a family portrait dating from 1911. Frans must be the chubby toddler in a white lace dress sitting on his mother's lap. She is a small woman with an attractive but stern face. His two sisters stand next to them, and alongside them, their father: tall and thin, with a large handlebar mustache. In the course of nineteen photographs, Frans progresses from a toddler to a dark, surly little boy, a teenager, a young man. The older he gets, the more distant his expression, almost unfriendly—or is that my imagination?

In addition to the family photos, there are dozens of pictures of landscapes, men in military garb, and cars. Lots of pictures of Frans as an adult posing as a dandy behind the wheel of a car, each time with a different woman next to him. From a distance you'd say he was good-looking: dark hair, ditto expression, a natty dresser. From close-up—for instance, on his driver's license, also part of the trove—his looks are just average: not homely, not handsome. A man you wouldn't notice without the cars and the outfits.

Do I really look like him, as K claimed? If I look closely, I do see certain likenesses. The same straight nose, the same narrow mouth. In most of the photos, Bommenneef appears to be on vacation: a suitcase tied to the roof rack, a snowcapped mountain or deserted beach in the background.

Underneath the photos is an envelope of divorce papers. In 1938, the marriage between Frans and a certain Carolina was annulled. They had only been married for two years. He got the sideboard, she the Persian rugs.

It's a strange sensation, going through this entirely unique and yet utterly unimportant find. How big was the chance that after seventy years, this very box would end up in my possession, the only person interested in the history behind the legend of Bommenneef? And yet, what on earth am I supposed to do with a pile of traffic tickets? What can his insurance papers tell me about the bombing? What good is a tax return when what I'm really after are the details of an act of heroism?

This box, all these papers, the hollowness of a humdrum life, make me uncomfortable. It's too intimate, too trivial, too disappointing. Where are the letters from the Resistance? Where are the medals? The proof of courage, sacrifice, and allegiance?

I try to trace the box's history. Who packed up his things shortly after the war, and why? Aunt S doesn't know; her son-in-law promises to look into it, but the trail runs dry with the collector who had bought the box at an auction but cannot remember from whom.

I recall something a historian friend once told me: less than 0.001 percent of everything that has been written down in the course of history survives. There are two things you don't find in historical documents: that which, at the time, was common knowledge, and that which no one wanted mentioned.

FIVE DAYS NOW with no news about Bommenneef. The grapevine has gone quiet, the elderly have returned to their bridge evenings, and I sit here with stacks of traffic tickets and vacation snapshots.

I try to concentrate on the deadlines I need to meet before the baby arrives. Following the advice of friends with children— pretty soon you won't have any time for each other!—D and I do things together. It's a weirdly indeterminate togetherness. We treat each other like ex-lovers. Friendly, careful, with the understanding that nothing will ever be as it was. Sometimes we talk about the baby, but these are brief, routine conversations. What is there to say about someone who doesn't exist yet? Sometimes people ask me if I already love my child. I don't know how to respond. The thing that's growing inside me does not feel like a child. More like a restless organ. It's like being asked if I love my liver. So the honest answer is: no, but I wouldn't want to live without it either.

The news lapse on Bommenneef makes me fidgety. The traces of information I saw dotting the empty white map these past weeks made me feel in control. But now, the empty landscape is once again encroaching on my thoughts. D says I should concentrate on the life that's on its way, rather than on a life that has passed. But I no longer seem to be able to separate the two.

My quest is starting to irritate him. Our quibbling invariably ends up at the same bone of contention: D says it's "just a name." To which I reply that a name is always more than a name. A memory, for example, the first and biggest one you're given.

"It's a word," D says.

"It's a foothold," I say.

"It says nothing about who he'll become."

"It says everything about what I want him to become."

We ping-pong back and forth like this until D throws his hands in the air, as though beseeching some higher entity, and, shaking his head, throws in the towel. Not because he admits I'm right, but because he has read somewhere that there's no point arguing with a pregnant woman.

I try to link up the snippets of information I've collected so far; I seek out the most logical route from the little boy on the donkey cart to the man who orchestrated a bombing. They are all dead-end roads.

Just when I'm starting to lose faith, I get a telephone call. The woman on the line identifies herself as B, "the best friend Frans ever had." The grapevine was apparently not entirely dormant: this morning she heard about my search via an acquaintance who was a friend of a nephew of a cousin, et cetera. B has a thin, high-pitched voice, and she gasps after every sentence, as though she's climbing a staircase as we talk, but she's sitting down—at least, that's what she says when she calls: "I've been sitting here in my chair thinking, ever since I heard that a niece of Frans was looking for information." I should come see her in The Hague as soon as I can, she tells me.

"Is tomorrow soon enough?"

She laughs. "Fine. I'm always available, it's one of the benefits of being old."

D thinks I should first check whether she really knew Bommenneef that well. "You need your rest. You don't want to make that whole trip for nothing." But who would I ask? I've yet to speak to anyone who knew Frans well enough to know about his inner circle.

I decide not to expect too much from this meeting. If B is about the same age as Frans, then she'd be about a hundred now. There's a good chance her memory has clouded over.

But no, B is as sharp as a tack. She is nearly ninety, and quite beautiful, with big dark eyes and a gray bun of hair that glistens like fresh fish. "Inscrutable" is the word that pops into my head when she opens the door. Everywhere in her apartment are portraits of the same three faces: her husband, her son, her grandson. She smiles as I enter. "Good to have a Van Heemstra drop by again. Frans was part of the family."

I smile back, relieved. Finally, someone who really knew

Bommenneef. Impatient to get to the heart of the matter, I wrestle my way through a slice of apple pie and the usual first-encounter small talk. When she gets up to fetch some more pie, I ask her what she can tell me about the attack.

She raises her eyebrows. "The attack?"

I nod.

"You mean that bomb thing?"

"Yes," I say. "That bomb thing."

She brushes off my words.

"I don't know anything about that. I only met Frans in the fifties—at the racetrack my husband used to frequent."

What she does know for certain is that he was convicted and sent to jail in Leeuwarden in 1947. She confirms the story that Juliana gave him a royal pardon. She reckons he served about three years in total.

For two hours, I ask and B answers. It is a strange conversation that seems to be going nowhere. I have the sensation that we are talking in circles, that I'm only seeing the periphery of Bommenneef's story, because B never gives me a straight answer.

Me: How did he come into contact with the Resistance?

B: The Resistance came into contact with him.

Me: Did he murder many people during the war?

B: Is a murder in wartime still a murder?

Me: Was the bombing a murder?

B: According to the judge, yes.

Me: And according to you?

B: I'll go make some more tea.

Out of all her dodging I am able to distill the following:

Frans's shoes were always worn out. Whenever there was no woman in his life, B picked out his clothes for him. She loved knotting his ties, then running her fingers through his hair like a comb. She met Frans at the Zandvoort racecourse, where he and his friends watched the races, or even took part himself, for instance against his best friend, Maurice Schulp. Maurice was also the brother of Frans's second wife, Nelly, whom he married in 1950, while still in prison.

The racecourse attracted people who—B hesitates briefly as she says this—wanted to *live*. She says it emphatically.

Frans once told her that he didn't hate the Nazis because of their ideology per se but resented them taking over his country. But he didn't mean it as crudely as it sounds, B says when I ask, shocked, if he really said that. He had a lifelong issue with authority, she explained, which the Germans' jackboots and stinging orders only exacerbated. According to B, Frans was "duped" into taking part in that Sinterklaas Eve attack. By whom, and why, remains unclear. (Me: By who, then? She: The others. Me: Why? She: That's just how it went. Me: How did it go? She: The way it did.) In prison, some of his cellmates had been conscientious objectors, men who refused to go fight in the Dutch East Indies. He couldn't stand those "leftist idiots," B utters with such acerbity that I am afraid she had looked up my politically correct profile on the internet.

But she's already switched subjects: Frans's women. Bad choices, the lot of them. The first wife, Carolina, was a Nazi sympathizer; the second one, Nelly, was young and reckless. They started a relationship shortly after the war and got married after the bombing. If anyone knew anything about the bomblet, it was Nelly, B says, but Nelly is dead. Her voice contains a whiff of triumph at the word "dead." Frans's third wife (B cannot, or does not want to, remember her name) took him to Vinaròs, Spain, where it was so scorching hot in the summer that he spent weeks on end lying on his bed under the ceiling fan. When the nameless wife died a few years later, he stayed on, alone. He chain-smoked, and when he wasn't smoking, he coughed. In his last years, he was gradually consumed by diabetes. B was there when they amputated Frans's legs in the hospital in Nijmegen. She hired a nurse to care for him in Spain, but she quit after a few months because he wanted more from her than just medical care.

And so it went with subsequent nurses as well. He got the short end of the stick, B says—as if the victims weren't the women, but poor, legless, needy Frans under the ceiling fan.

After an extensive search, B says, they managed to find an ex-marine who agreed to move in and care for him. Frans spent his last months in the arms of the bald, burly seaman, who moved him between bed and wheelchair, and bathed him whenever Frans allowed it, which was seldom.

Then the marine would phone B: "The captain won't take his bath."

Sometimes she would go to Spain to care for him herself and found he had been wearing the same clothes for months.

B wrote regularly, but Frans never wrote back.

Whenever she visited, all he wanted to talk about was car racing.

She knows little about the bombing except that the man who was killed was a collaborator, and therefore had it coming.

The story about Frans swimming across a river with a knife in his teeth vaguely rings a bell, but she's forgotten whom she heard it from, and when.

Her long monologue leaves me feeling disoriented.

The women, the cars, the marine—red herrings.

I want to understand his act of heroism, the moment he put it all on the line, the mindset it reflects.

B rises to make more tea.

A hero is someone who got away with being reckless.

Who wrote that again? Hermans. *The Darkroom of Damocles.*

But Bommenneef didn't get away with it. He sacrificed his freedom for his principles.

B returns from the kitchen with a wood-framed certificate. "I found this while cleaning out the house in Vinaròs after the funeral. He was given it right after the war; it's a commendation for his work in the Resistance. It really belongs in the family, so here, please have it." As I take it, she runs her finger over the ring on my hand. "He wore it day and night."

I can't quite read her expression. Melancholy? Yearning? She says that Frans was a good man, *no matter what*—she says that last bit in English, with an exaggerated British accent.

The frame contains a yellowed document, its text in faded block letters. *With this Certificate of Service I record my appreciation of the aid rendered by . . . as a volunteer in the service of the United Nations or the great cause of Freedom.* Frans's name is written in brown ink on the preprinted dotted line.

In the lower right corner is the dark-blue signature of Field Marshal Montgomery, the renowned British war hero. A row of elegant curls with a short flourish at the end. I get out of my chair, carefully put the frame into my bag, and thank B. This is what I was looking for. Proof of heroism. Something that makes the traffic tickets and stale gossip pale by comparison.

When I get home, I hammer a nail into the wall of the baby nursery and hang the certificate above the foot of the cradle, in full view of my son-to-be.

D, TOO, IS impressed by the dark-blue signature. Just yesterday he mockingly referred to my quest as a "retirement home national tour," but now he gazes admiringly at the certificate on the wall.

"I had no idea it was such a big deal."

I glow with pride, as if Bommenneef were my very own son, not some distant uncle I'd never met.

D asks what my next step is.

"Maybe this is it," I reply. I've spoken to everyone familiar with the incident, and according to B, all his other close acquaintances are dead by now. I think back on what she said as I was leaving. "Frans was a good man, no matter what." It's a tidy-sounding conclusion. A good person. And a framed citation to prove it.

"But this can't be everything, can it?" D exclaims. "Just look at that signature! This is the kind of stuff that becomes a bestseller. And you don't write a bestseller by chitchatting over coffee with well-meaning family. This story deserves better. If you're going to do it, then do it right."

A few months ago I would probably have been irritated by his comments, but now his sudden encouragement does me good. It feels like we haven't had a normal conversation in days. Sometimes I think it's my belly: the bigger it gets, the less we talk. As though there's not much else to say, now that the cards have been dealt. He a father, me a mother, end of story.

"I already googled the bombing long ago and didn't get any hits."

"There are other ways."

"Such as?" I sound more eager than I'd like to.

D smiles the way you smile at a dimwitted child.

"For starters, this was covered in the newspapers, so it must be archived somewhere." He reaches for his telephone and types a message. "I'll text Stefan, he works at a news desk. He'll know where to look for this kind of thing." One second later his telephone pings. He walks over to the dining room table, flips open his laptop, types something in, and stares at the screen, his eyes wide.

"Wow." He whistles softly.

"What?" I walk over to the table, try to commandeer the laptop, but he pulls it closer.

"This was *huge*! Front-page news!"

"Where?"

"Everywhere. 'The Sinterklaas Murders,' 'Bloody Gift Night.' This is a James Bond film!"

"Lemme see."

He turns his laptop toward me. The browser shows a website of online newspaper archives with eleven full pages of links to articles about the bombing. Why didn't this ever occur to me? I look at D, too flabbergasted to say anything. He grins and mouths the word *am-a-teur*.

I take the laptop upstairs and sit down at my desk. In five hours I've read all 132 articles about the bombing that appeared between December 1946 and June 1948. Then I reread them. And reread them again. It's as though a snowbank is melting before my very eyes, revealing the glistening contours of a bigger story than I'd ever imagined. Bigger—far bigger—than the compact myth it has become.

On December 5, 1946, an army vehicle tears southward down the Rijksweg in The Hague, heading for Brussels. At the wheel is the thirty-seven-year-old Captain Frans van Heemstra. Most of the newspapers presume he had an explosive with him intended for a Belgian target. One or two journalists cast doubt on this theory, because no bomb went off in Brussels and there is no indication that an attack had been planned in the Belgian capital. Frans has the road to himself. Gasoline is still rationed and cars are scarce, but as the head of the motor vehicle facility at the army base in The Hague he has access to the fleet of military vehicles. The weather: partly cloudy, some sun, then wet snow. Temperature: just above freezing. Evening is approaching. Across the country, fathers are sneaking out of the house to change into their St. Nicholas disguises.

A few hours earlier, Frans handed a list of addresses to two of his subordinates, Corporal Peterse and Sergeant Haastrecht. It is a hit list, the names of the four men who are to be liquidated that evening.

The bombs to be used had been assembled by one Corporal De Boer. "Hellish machines," writes the *Utrechts Nieuwsblad*. They're small wooden boxes about the size of a pound cake, each containing a hand grenade and a wine bottle filled with gasoline. When the box is opened, the bottle shifts, pressing against the grenade's detonating mechanism. Four seconds later there is an explosion, igniting the fuel-filled wine bottle. The explosives are wrapped up to look like Sinterklaas presents. Peterse has scribbled "From St. Nick" on them. They're tied with ribbons.

While Frans is heading for Brussels, Sergeant Haastrecht is riding his motorcycle toward Amsterdam with one of the explosives in his saddlebag. He has a passenger behind him, a fellow sergeant who had nothing further to do with the story. His involvement is purely coincidental: he was hitchhiking, a shivering soldier at the side of the road hoping to get a lift home. Everything would have gone differently if Haastrecht hadn't picked him up, but he is a friendly sort, or a loyal one (you don't leave a fellow soldier stranded at the side of the road), or a reckless one, or a stupid one, or perhaps simply a terrified sergeant who has been trembling with panic all those kilometers on his motorbike with that deadly payload in his bag. Four seconds till detonation isn't much time—one pothole and you're a goner.

But that first second goes by without Haastrecht noticing. The wobbling weight of the hitchhiker shifts the bag, which in turn makes the wine bottle slide, and for those next three seconds Haastrecht makes no moves to escape, because he still has no idea until—*four, three, two, one*—they are catapulted into the air, the motorbike flips, and shrapnel, flames, and limbs skitter across the asphalt.

Haastrecht lands some distance from the motorbike, and he miraculously escapes the flames and chunks of metal. He scrambles to his feet, only slightly injured, and makes a run for it. An hour later a passerby finds his passenger at the side of the road, wounded and unconscious. When he comes to, he provides the police with a description of the driver. Haastrecht is the first to be arrested the following day.

Around the time Haastrecht's bomb explodes, the twenty-eight-year-old Corporal Peterse, Frans's second subordinate, stops two passersby on the Prinsengracht in The Hague. He asks if they would deliver a Sinterklaas surprise to number 266. They take the parcel and ring the bell at the address. When the door opens, they set it on the steps and shout up the stairs, "From St. Nick! From St. Nick!"

They amble briefly on, until they hear a boom and the sound of breaking glass. When they look back, they see a cloud of dust and smoke rising from the house they had just called at. A burning curtain flaps "like a large red torch" out of the window.

Corporal Peterse likewise sees the torch. He has parked his motorbike at the end of the street to make sure the bomb has reached its target. But the thundering explosion gives him second thoughts about the whole operation. When he gets to Delft, the home of the next two targets, he stops at a canal and—splosh, splosh—drops both parcels into the water, one at a time. Then Peterse gets back on his motorbike and rides home, to bed, to the arms of his wife, who a few days later is quoted in the newspaper as saying that his hair smelled of gunpowder that night, and that, for the first time since she'd known him, he cried in his sleep.

Haastrecht and Peterse and bomb-maker De Boer are all puppets of Frans, who is fingered as "the brain behind the bombings." They knew each other from the Resistance and had been stationed at the same army garrison in The Hague. According to the newspapers, for months Frans had fed them reports of Dutch collaborators who had evaded justice, and insisted they needed to take matters into their own hands, because otherwise it would all have been for naught, the years of Resistance and risking their lives in the belief that the postwar Netherlands would become a different, better place. He spoke (according to one weekly magazine) of a "shadow army" and that they yearned to "carry on with the resistance" once peace came. Van Heemstra knew the men would go all out for him and would not shy away from using extreme violence. De Boer, for instance, is said to have single-handedly killed six German soldiers at Apeldoorn station during the war. He shot some of them point-blank, the others he strangled with his bare hands. He then dragged the bodies to an empty locomotive, which he then set on fire.

The soldiers were quick to embrace their captain's plans. They had enough weapons to unleash a new war. In De Boer's shed, police discovered machine guns, loaded pistols, crates full of ammunition, hand grenades, and rifles.

No one knows where Van Heemstra delivered his deadly cargo, if there even was one, or what he did afterward in Brussels.

There was speculation that others were involved with the bombings, but no proof for this was found.

The bomb on the Prinsengracht destroyed the upper floor. Three people died.

21 WEEKS LEFT

THREE FATALITIES. NOT just one "bomblet" but four, maybe even five hefty explosives. Not a solitary act, but a larger scheme that dominated the front pages for weeks. Now that the story covers a larger terrain than I had imagined, I need a new scale, new surveying instruments. D says we're bound to find somebody who wants to make it into a film. I counter that I need to know everything first. And besides, I don't want a film, I want a name. I wrestle with the new words that have been appended to the story. "Hit list." "Hellish machines." "Strangle."

While I try to think through my strategy for the coming weeks, I'm being devoured by everything that needs to be done. I read and write, visit friends' babies, go into town with my parents to buy a stroller. They're surprised by the newspaper articles, but not as much as I had expected. "These things are always a lot messier than you think," says my father. War, he means. Violence.

I ask him how it's possible that I've never heard this version before. Didn't anyone read the newspapers back then? How could this story have been magically transformed into our tidy, straightforward family legend?

"It's just how families work." He shrugs. "Like that game of telephone. Stories get whispered from generation to generation, and what comes out at the other end is always different than what went in." I suppose so, but it's not a game I want to play with my son. I want to tell him the whole, true story, loud and clear.

I call B and ask her where on earth she came up with just one person getting killed that evening.

"That's what I was told," she says.

I tell her what was in the newspapers.

It's quiet on the other end of the line.

"I don't know anything about that."

"So were there three collaborators in that one house?"

"I only know what I was told: that one Blackshirt got killed."

"Did Frans tell you that?"

"Frans never talked about it. The story circulated."

"Always the same story?"

"Always the same."

"And now?" It's more a question for myself than for her.

"Now it's another story," she replies dryly.

The newspapers offer no information about the fatalities. No names or ages, no interviews with witnesses or next of kin.

The reporting stops at the front door of number 266. I make a separate Casualties document in the Facts folder on my desktop. For now it contains only one word: "three." I go through the various possibilities. The most logical one seems that there had been a get-together of a group of former Blackshirts that night on the Prinsengracht. That the bomb killed not just one turncoat, but a whole gang of them. I prefer to leave the other possibilities—innocent victims, bad timing—out of the equation.

D shouts from the bedroom. When I get upstairs, I see him standing on the bed, waving a folded-up newspaper. The place is swarming with mosquitoes. I look around the room, see them dancing in the light of the bedside lamp. They're on the cupboards, the walls, the window sash—it's as though our bedroom has been hit by a Biblical plague. There are two large blood smears on the expensive palm-print wallpaper. "I've never seen anything like it," D says. He winds up again, swings, and splat!—a bloodstain on the white ceiling.

"Must be the combination of the rain and the heat," I say.

"This means war," D says as he hands me half the newspaper.

I stand next to him on the bed and swat at a fat, dark one next to the window. I miss.

I ask him who he thinks the three fatalities were.

He scowls, then shrugs his shoulders.

"One traitor plus collateral damage."

"Don't be so cynical."

"It happens to the best of them."

"I can't imagine Bommenneef sacrificing two innocent people for the sake of one collaborator."

"How many innocent lives do you think those drones of our

hero Obama have cost? How many people have been sacrificed to catch one terrorist?"

I shake my head. "It must have been three collaborators."

"Does it matter?" D whacks the ceiling with the newspaper.

I look at the blood spatters. In primary school I had a friend who came from Den Helder, way up north, and she told me that they used to refer to the mosquitoes as "cousins," because after they bit you, they were blood relatives. I swat at two dancing cousins near my shoulder. I miss again.

"Of course it matters!"

"If you're so dead set on him being the perfect hero, then maybe you should stop looking." D swats again, with success, but two new cousins alight in the bloodbath. For every dead mosquito, ten living ones seem to take its place.

"How can I, if I know the story's not true?"

"There are so many stories that aren't entirely true. But if they're good stories, ones we want to pass down, then what's the problem?"

A mosquito zooms past my ear, bites me in the neck, I swat, but only hit myself.

Another one bites me, this time in the leg. I flail wildly with the newspaper.

D laughs at me. "You're supposed to kill them, not dance for them."

I search for an answer to D's question—whether a story has to be exactly true—but my thoughts run aground in the dark muck of hormones, fatigue, buzzing.

Perhaps the stories we tell ourselves don't need to be perfect, as long as they assist us in some way, if they make us happier, give us confidence in ourselves and in mankind. Why nitpick about the details? A bit from a book I read recently—Coetzee, I think—comes to mind; it says that we put so much stock in the complete truth, no matter how ugly it is, because we're convinced that life proceeds according to a dramaturgic plan. We see it as an arc from A to B, with some obligatory demon-wrestling along the way. The logic of drama, of the novel, demands that we not banish the truth, but come to terms with it. It requires conflict and an internal struggle, and then a "good" ending. That is the arc we are meant to, or want to, traverse. We seek out drama in order to vanquish it.

But life is not a novel, writes Coetzee (yes, it was Coetzee, I looked it up, *The Good Story*); thousands of things are suppressed, tidied up, or forgotten without anybody losing even a second of sleep over it. Coetzee would say that D is right, that there's no earthly reason to rake up every last detail of this story, to map out the entire truth. Unless you want to turn it into a novel.

20 WEEKS LEFT

W HAT I NOW know for sure: on December 5, 1946, a parcel bomb disguised as a Sinterklaas gift was delivered to Prinsengracht 266 in The Hague. Three people were killed. Three other bombs never reached their destination. Bommenneef drove to Brussels that evening, possibly with a fourth explosive, heading for an as-yet-unknown target. These are my known coordinates. In between them is a maze of slippery paths—the possibilities—and a few slightly more navigable routes—the probabilities. Surrounding all this: large, blank, white patches.

I think of the cartographer of that empty map of Antarctica. Did someone else determine how much emptiness should be shown? Did they discuss whether this or that uncharted region should be included? How do you map the unknown? The starting point, the cartographer's first question, is of course what scale to use. 1:whatever.

If I had the time, if the cells in my womb were not multiplying like crazy, then I'd want to find and spend some more time with those passersby in The Hague. I would revisit number 266 with them, listen to the statement they gave at the police station, follow them home through the darkened city, back along the street they sauntered unsuspectingly along just a few hours earlier. I tried to imagine how it felt when they got home, what they told their families, how they untied the ribbons on their own Sinterklaas gifts, the explosion of a few hours prior still reverberating in their ears. Could they simply join in with the songs and the treats, or were their thoughts dominated all evening by vexing questions and nagging suppositions? What if they had said no? What if the bomb had gone off too soon? What if, what if . . .

If I had the time, I would follow all the side paths the newspaper articles take. I'd climb aboard the fire truck that put out the blaze, mingle with the shocked neighbors crowding the sidewalk after the explosion, sit at the bedside of the injured hitchhiker during his monthslong recuperation. I would find out who else was on the hit list, and why.

But I don't have time for detours—the avocado is quickly becoming "as long as a toothbrush." It has fingernails, it can distinguish between light and dark, and who knows what all else.

I must stick to Bommenneef. Questions aplenty. Who was his potential target in Brussels? And why didn't the bomb go off?

The newspapers offer no answers. But surely Frans took someone into his confidence at the time. I google the surnames Peterse and Haastrecht, but the online phone book alone contains hundreds of them. It will take more than the next twenty weeks to call them all. And De Boer: forget it.

I think of "reckless" Nelly Schulp, Bommenneef's second wife, who was his partner after the war. Perhaps there is still some family left who might know something, children from a later marriage, perhaps, with whom she shared things about her time with Frans. The surname Schulp is less common than Peterse or De Boer. Within an hour I've called all the Schulps in the phone book, and have spoken to about half of them, with no luck. As for the others, I leave voice mail messages, I write emails and search Facebook profiles. Two days later I've spoken to twenty-eight Schulps, from Friesland to Limburg. But no one remembers Nelly.

We're halfway there. According to 24baby.nl, our son is now the size of a winter carrot and weighs as much as a pair of flip-flops—a strange combination of seasons that corresponds to my disoriented state of mind. I finish assignments, see friends, visit family, go to the theater, but I feel disconnected. It's as though I'm out of sync with everyday life, with the day that becomes night, the performance that comes to a close, the deadline that is met. Mine is a different time zone; *here* is only exponential growth. A big bang in slow motion.

In the waiting room of the ultrasound clinic, D and I get into a tiff when he finds out that the scan we're here for today has nothing to do with Down syndrome screening, that this possibility is seven weeks behind us already, and that I decided on my own not to have it done. It wasn't actually even a conscious decision; I just let the moment pass and didn't mention it, knowing he would never think of it himself.

I don't have a strong opinion about prenatal screenings, I just didn't feel like yet more fussing around my abdomen. The appointment before ours is running late. The couple after us is already here. The woman has a pointy belly and a flushed complexion. Her eyes glisten as though she's got a fever. She smiles at me the way pregnant women smile at each other. Conspiratorial. *Just look at all these fools here, obsessed with the present, while we waddlers, filled with the future, are worth twice as much as these singletons.*

D is furious. "If things go wrong, it's your fault," he snaps at me. "You knew and should have told me."

"I knew and I didn't want it. It was my decision."

"And so you decided for me."

"You decided for yourself, by not being on top of things."

But D doesn't buy it. According to him, everything that has to do with the baby is my responsibility. It's my job to keep him posted, ask for help if it gets too much for me, remind him of appointments and tests.

Ever since the results of the pregnancy test came in, I have been the designated project manager of this enterprise. D is at most an enthusiastic employee who clocks in and out at will.

Ten minutes later, when the technician says that everything looks fine, D's anger has subsided. The blotches from a few weeks ago have grown into something that is starting to look like a person. In the semidarkness of my belly floats another belly with two arms, two legs, a neck, and a disproportionately large head that jerks along the edge of the ultrasound image. He's got hiccups, the obstetrician says.

Hiccups, D repeats, his voice full of admiration. I look at him as he looks at the image, proud of his son's hiccups. The jerky movements make me uneasy, it's as though the baby wants to get out, away from me, into the world.

On the way home I see I've got one missed call from an unknown number. There's a Schulp on my voice mail: the son of Maurice, the car racer, Frans's best friend, Nelly's brother. I return the call as soon as we get home.

"Nelly is my aunt," he confirms. "I don't know much about her, we're not what you'd call a close family, but I seem to remember she had a son in Zeeland."

I go over to my desk and glance through the list of Schulps. The only phone number in Zeeland was for a car mechanic, and there was no answer. As soon as Maurice's son has hung up, I redial the Zeeland number.

It rings four times, and then a woman's voice answers. I rattle off the story that I've rattled off for dozens of Schulps over the last few days. About Bommenneef, the ring, the attack, that I'm trying to trace the Nelly who married Frans van Heemstra in 1950.

"Family of the captain?" the woman asks. She's got a faint Rotterdam accent and an upbeat voice. "I think she might have mentioned it before."

My heart skips a beat. This could be the source I've been looking for.

"Are you her daughter?"

"Daughter-in-law."

"And she told you about the captain?"

The woman is quiet. "It was a long time ago," she says hesitantly.

My enthusiasm sags. "Might your husband know more about it?"

"Maybe if you dropped by . . ."

I'm of two minds. I don't feel like traveling all the way to Zeeland for nothing.

"Is there a diary, maybe?" I ask. "Or letters?"

"Nelly would know that better than I."

"Nelly's *alive*?" I do my best not to scream the question.

NELLY IS STILL alive.

A few days after this discovery, I sit facing her on the veranda of a service apartment in Vlissingen. It's a cold summer day. The coffee is lukewarm, the cream puffs we bought in the commissary seem to have come straight from the freezer. I'm exhausted; the mosquito invasion has gotten worse by the day. D has bought an electric insect killer in the form of a tennis racket. I lie there at night, swatting with it for hours on end. Hit one and a small flash of light shoots through the wire mesh. The bigger the mosquito, the bigger the flash. Sometimes it leaves behind the stench of burned flesh. I got a fright the first time I smelled it. I remembered learning in biology class that only female mosquitoes bite, and then only if they are ovulating. I wonder if it's the eggs I smell burning, and how many generations of mosquitoes I've annihilated with that one swipe. But once I got over the squeamishness, it became addictive: retribution for all those sleepless hours. Roasted mosquito became the smell of vengeance.

There is a large red welt under my left eye that makes my face looked lopsided, but I don't think Nelly sees it. In fact, I don't think Nelly sees much at all. Her eyes are buried under a thick agglomeration of baggy skin. She seems to feel her way around.

Nelly still has a stately posture even though she no longer walks completely erect. She is wearing a colorful batik blouse, and her cheeks are dark and smooth, like polished wood. Her voice is so raspy that I have to hold my ear right up close to her lips in order to catch her words before they vanish into the chilly summer air. It must be a strange sight, as though I'm offering her my cheek, waiting for a kiss.

Nelly's memories of Frans are similar to B's: women, cars, disdain for anything leftist. "Frans was a hunter. Not the kind of man a person should be married to."

They never had children because he had contracted the mumps just before the war, which rendered him sterile. "But he could never accept that it was because of him. Maybe that's why he was always on the prowl, hoping that there was some woman out there who it would succeed with after all."

I ask her about the bombing, whether she knew anything about the preparations.

She shakes her head. "Frans wasn't a talker, and that suited me."

"But surely you questioned him after he'd been arrested?"

"He said he was innocent."

"And that was enough for you?"

She nods. After that, she dismisses all my questions about the bombing.

"I hardly know anything about it."

What she does know is who the target was at Prinsengracht 266: a Mr. Boer.

I assume she's confusing him with corporal De Boer, the one who made the bombs, but Nelly shakes her head when I bring him up.

"No, no, that was *De* Boer," she insists. "This was Boer. Just Boer. He had to be killed."

"Why?"

"Something to do with Engelandvaarders, I think." She looks at me questioningly, not entirely certain of her answer. "He had betrayed someone to the authorities. Or maybe more people."

"And the others who were killed?"

"Were there others?"

A chilly wind blows across the otherwise empty veranda. I shiver, zip up my coat. Nelly is oblivious to it all. She picks crumbs from her plate with her long, dark fingers. A tropical bird under the pale Zeeland sky.

"Do you have any idea who the target was in Brussels?"

Nelly springs to life, smiles broadly.

"He was on his way to see *me* that night. We had quarreled— for the umpteenth time—there was another woman. Frans took these things . . . rather lightly. I said to him: now it's really over. And I left for Brussels. I went to work as an au pair for this awful family. I regretted it terribly, but I was too proud to go back. I wanted him to miss me, to come looking for me. And that evening, out of the blue, he appeared at the door."

She laughs. A low, dusty sound.

"Pack your bags, he said, and I did. We slept in the Hotel De Goudfazant, downtown. It was wonderful."

"Could you tell if he had any explosives with him?"

"He had a valise with pajamas and cigarettes. No more than that."

"Was he nervous that evening? Depressed?"

She shakes her head. "He was relaxed," she says. "Dressed to the nines and in good humor." She hadn't noticed anything unusual about him. But, she adds, nothing could rattle Frans. Not even the morning after their romantic tryst, when Nelly's brother Maurice appeared downstairs in the hotel lobby. He had dropped in to visit his sister and was told that Frans had taken her away the previous night.

Maurice looked from his younger sister to his friend, and then said threateningly, "So, Frans, what're we going to do?" And Frans, perfectly cool, answered, "Get married."

Nelly and Frans drove back to Amsterdam, their hands intertwined around the gear shift. When they arrived, the police were waiting for them, and a day later Frans was taken into custody. They were only able to wed two years after his conviction—in the Leeuwarden prison chapel.

Nelly chuckles.

"Wouldn't you know it, I had a great big pimple on my nose that day. I wore a secondhand dress with a coffee stain on it, and we hadn't any rings."

So Frans slid his own ring onto her middle finger—my ring, the ring I got from my grandmother. Nelly touches the stone with a long, sinewy finger.

"I wore it until the day I left him for good, in the spring

of '58; I remember ripping it off and throwing it at his head."

She looks silently at the blue stone for a moment, and I feel myself becoming uneasy. What if she wants it back? Should I give it to her?

Fortunately, she resumes her story.

"He had a hard time of it in prison. When I came to visit, he complained that he had to fight off the other men, and he detested the conscientious objectors he had to share a cell with. He thought pacifists were dangerous fools. A man is meant to fight for his country, was his motto. He was afraid that every generation after the war would become progressively softer. He was angry about so many things. In fact, he was always angry." She gingerly places a hand on the half-frozen cream puff, as though to protect it from the cold summer.

I ask if she still bears a grudge against him. She shakes her head. "Life with Frans was a ball. When he wasn't angry, he sang, all day long. We would sit till all hours in cafés with the Canadians. Sometimes we spent the whole weekend in bed. Those were bleak years for me, and Frans cheered them up. The only thing I couldn't take was that cheating of his. And also, during and after the war, his obsessive, pathological planning for the next battle."

One day, when she snapped at him that the war was really and truly over, Frans asked: How long does a war last, then?

Until peace comes, Nelly replied. He just laughed at her.

"It's funny," she says, "but some things just stick in your mind your whole life long. That one night in De Goudfazant— that was worth everything. It was pure happiness. From beginning to end. It was—" She cuts herself short.

I feel it's indiscreet to ask more about that night. A long, awkward silence follows. I thumb through my notebook, as though consulting my notes on how this conversation is supposed to continue. Out of the corner of my eye, I see Nelly wolf down her cream puff.

I ask if she regrets having left Frans.

"It seemed like the right decision at the time."

When we say goodbye, Nelly takes one last look at the ring. "It would never fit me now," she says.

Her eyes glisten, and suddenly I see how beautiful she is, with her long Indonesian face, and realize how attractive she must have been as a young woman. We say goodbye at the elevator. The doors slide shut with a sound that resembles a sigh, and I imagine her being teletransported to another era. Back to the past, whence she materialized.

In the lobby of the apartment building my telephone rings. It's D, asking if we could reschedule tomorrow's appointment with the obstetrician. I ask him why he doesn't just call her himself.

"You've got the number."

"It's online."

"But you've got it on your phone."

"I'll text it to you."

"Why do you always have to make things so complicated?"

"It's easy. I send you the number, and you call."

"That's so roundabout."

He's right, it is roundabout. I don't send him the number. Just like I did not send him the numbers of the ultrasound clinic and the postnatal care. I wonder where exactly our paths diverged; how I ended up along the route of all the practical baby matters, while somewhere off in the distance, he meanders through his days.

I send him a text.

I miss you.

I get it. Hang in there, in a couple of hours I'm all yours.

I respond with a smiley. Closeness won't make me miss him any less, probably only more. In the train from Vlissingen to Amsterdam I examine my face in the reflection of the window. My head looks swollen, not just because of that bug bite. I've gained more than four pounds in the past week; the obstetrician says it's mostly fluids. My ankles and wrists are thicker than ever, water reservoirs are forming around my joints, sometimes I imagine I hear myself sloshing. I look at the notes I took during my conversation with Nelly. They don't even fill a full page. A few sentences, a couple of keywords. In the middle of the page I've written Brussels! At least now I know why Bommenneef went there. Not for a liquidation, but for love. A new pushpin on the map. Only thing is, it doesn't exactly bring me closer to heroism. While Peterse lay in bed crying next to his wife and Haastrecht was injured and on the run, Frans spent the night in a swanky hotel with his sweetheart. Maybe she was his alibi that evening. Maybe his bomb also went off too early, although Nelly said he looked spruce. I take a pen from my bag and change the exclamation mark after Brussels to a question mark.

The baby kicks. For the first time, I yearn to see him and to touch him. It is a large, all-encompassing yearning.

I look around; the compartment is empty.

I lay my chin on my chest, direct my voice at my belly, and start to talk. Ridiculous, but it feels good. "I don't know who you are or who you'll become, what you expect, what I should say to you when you're here. I don't even know how to hold you. But I'm working on a story. Your first story. I promise you it'll be a good one, the best first story a boy can have. It's got war in it, and peace, a hero and a villain; it works, just like a song you can sing along with after hearing it just once. You can come out once it's finished." Another kick. Deal.

I enter all the new information I got from Nelly into the search field on the computer. Boer + Informer + Engeland-vaarders.

As the page slowly loads, I watch the Zeeland landscape pass. There's nowhere to hide, nowhere to get lost. Flat fields, low trees. The connection keeps getting broken. Hopeless.

Only after the town of Goes does the internet reconnect. There is just one hit that contains all three keywords: a website with historical information about Ockenburgh Estate, situated between Loosduinen and Kijkduin, near the dunes in The Hague. The extensive historical overview includes two paragraphs about the occupation. The beach and vicinity were heavily patrolled by the German coast guard, and it was off limits between nine at night and dawn. Twice, boats tried to leave Ockenburgh for England. They were intercepted both times.

And then, there he is, in the last paragraph. Boer. The informer.

In 1942, Mr. Boer is said to have lured twelve Engelandvaarders to his bird-trapping grounds at Ockenburgh Estate. The area was then cordoned off by German forces, and the next day it was announced that the Engelandvaarders had been betrayed and subsequently arrested. One of the German officers was said to have been decorated for his role in the arrests and had supposedly recommended Boer for a distinction as well for exposing the Engelandvaarders. It was said that after the war, Boer also had contact with SS officers who had gone into hiding. After liberation, the Political Investigations Unit in The Hague had begun an inquiry into Boer's activities, but there was insufficient evidence to pursue it. On 5 December 1946, a parcel bomb disguised as a Sinterklaas gift was delivered to Boer's residence in The Hague. When the package was opened, a violent explosion followed, instantly killing François Guillaume Jacques Boer. Two other persons present in the house later died of their injuries. The explosion caused a fire in the house, injuring three persons, including Boer's daughter-in-law. The attack appears to have been carried out in retaliation for the betrayal of the Ockenburgh Engelandvaarders.

As I read the article, I feel childishly triumphant: a man who betrayed twelve innocent people must not be allowed to get away with it. *Boontje komt om zijn loontje.*

But when I reread the article, I am struck by that recurring "is said to." The German *is said to* have recommended Boer for a distinction. Boer *is said to* have had contact with ex–SS officers. Rumors. Likelihoods, but without proof.

And then there are the other two persons present, who later died of their injuries. "Persons present": that doesn't sound like Blackshirts or die-hard traitors, more like blameless bystanders. Family members, perhaps, like the daughter-in-law who, according to the article, was injured in the bombing.

The keywords "François Boer + Ockenburgh" bring up a

magazine article about the dunes in North Holland. There's a photograph of two men in a small wooden structure. *Two Bird-Catchers on the Trapping Grounds*, reads the caption, with their names underneath. One of them is François Boer. It goes on to say that the grounds—a large, empty field behind the structure—were the property of the other man in the picture, Dirk Hoos. The article says that Ockenburgh was well situated for catching finches, siskins, and starlings. Originally this was done for consumption, and, starting in 1936, "in the interest of migration studies." So Dirk and François caught birds, banded them, and set them free. The photograph is black-and-white and of poor quality; it is so pixilated that Dirk Hoos resembles the cartoonish Captain Haddock. He is wearing a dark Alpine hat, has a pipe in his mouth, and gazes off into the distance. Boer's appearance clashes with his adventurous-looking partner. He is dressed more like an office clerk than an outdoorsman. Trilby hat, starched collar, wool sweater, scarf, and snug-fitting jacket. He's holding a bundle of rope, perhaps a net. He, too, looks off into the distance, but it's a less distant distance than Dirk's. It is as though he's not quite sure where he's supposed to look. Alongside the seasoned outdoorsman with the cap and the pipe, he looks like the lackey who's allowed to hold the net and is just there to take up space in the photo. But maybe my opinion is colored by what I know, or what I want to know. Boer was indeed a dedicated birder: the article describes how they persevered in their bird banding "in the midst of the minefields." This article, too, ends with a reference to the bombing. "Mr. Boer died tragically in a liquidation on 5 December 1946, which is said to have been connected to collaboration during the war."

Said to.

Finding information about François Boer is easier than I thought. I follow D's friend Stefan's advice and consult the National Archive website. There is apparently a section called "Extraordinary Jurisdiction," which has a dossier on anyone who was subject to an investigation after the war under suspicion of collaboration. I send an email with François Boer's name and date of death, asking if there might be any information about him, and receive an answer within the hour. The dossier will be available for perusal in two days. I'm taken aback at the ease with which I—his killer's niece—am given access to François's dossier.

Two days later I go through the revolving door into the large main hall of "the nation's memory." I had expected a building packed with filing cabinets and ring binders; rooms full of diaries, photographs, testimonies, birth and death announcements: a stockpile of everything that is worth remembering. But here in the bare foyer, my overriding impression is that much has been forgotten. No binders, no bookshelves. A coffee bar off to the side, like a forgotten island in a sea of floor tiles. A small sign points to the Children's Book Museum, which shares the premises with the National Archive; one wrong turn and you're in the realm of fairy tales. The receptionist directs me to another counter, where I am given a pass and a pencil and sent to a third counter. The attendant there is a small man with sharp features, two deep, animalish eyes and a snout like an Afghan hound. I tell him my dossier number and he takes a cardboard box from the shelf behind him and slides it across the counter. I am to sit at the white table in the center of the reading room, he instructs me, which is reserved for those with dossiers from the Extraordinary Jurisdiction archives. I'm allowed to read everything, type it over if I want, but pictures and photocopies are strictly forbidden.

The white table is the only busy place in the otherwise quiet hall. I head for the last free seat. The box is lighter than I had expected, a paltry chronicle. I sit down, take out my laptop, and look at the brown cardboard. This could be the side path that leads me completely astray. Maybe I should focus on the heroes, and leave the victims be. But I can't get the words "said to" out of my head, and if I want to understand the *loontje* better, shouldn't I find out more about the *boontje*?

Across the table from me, a man of around seventy sits shaking his head above the papers spread out in front of him.

Next to him, two thin women—twins, I'm guessing—whisper quietly. Their faces are identical, as are their tidy white blouses; only the length of their stiff gray hair is different.

It looks like I'm the only under-fifty here. I figure most of them were born after the war and are now delving for stories about their parents, for whatever it was that was not talked about during all those dull postwar evenings of their youth.

A security man at the head of the table monitors us to make sure we stick to the rules and don't sneak any pictures. He walks over to me with two bright-pink Post-its: one for over the webcam on my laptop, one for my mobile phone. I never knew the privacy of dead people was so well guarded.

I place my hand on the box. There's something unbecoming about it, as though I'm about to open a grave. When I've removed the lid, I have to look twice before I see the dossier lying at the bottom. A thin folder the same color as the cardboard. It contains just a few loose sheets of paper.

"Military Authority, Political Investigative Unit's Gravenhage," it says on the first page. And then: "François Boer. Suspected of abetting the enemy." It is the report of the court case against François Boer. Three witnesses testified. The first, Leendert Vols, is also the man who made the initial accusation. He tells the judge that François worked at the Ockenburgh bird-trapping grounds during the war, and that shortly after the Dutch capitulation in 1940 he went into the city to catch pigeons for the Wehrmacht. Additionally, Vos had seen him fishing with a German and witnessed the catch being turned over at the end of the day to German officers billeted on the Laan van Nieuw Oost-Indië. "He brought the enemy fish and fowl."

Another witness stated that during the war, François had access to places "where no decent person was allowed." The third witness tells that François had permission to go to Rozenburg Island because his birds were kept there.

François's defense in the subsequent paragraph calls all these things "misunderstandings." The German fishing friend was a civilian resident and not a Nazi; nor was the fish ever delivered to officers. The police had instructed him to catch the pigeons—first with seeds soaked in genever, and when that did not work, with nets. He caught approximately two hundred. Not out of political motives, he says, but "because the police asked me to."

I reread the report. Then I inspect the pieces of evidence. Flimsy, creased bits of paper. Snippets that in those days could mean the difference between walking free or a life sentence. A *Sperrlinieausweis*, a *Sonderausweis*; I've no idea what the difference is, or in fact what they mean in the first place. D is right, I'm an amateur.

All those people seated at the table, hunched over their confidential dossiers with professional poise, their pencils at the ready, they nod knowingly above their folders, while I don't have the faintest idea where Rozenburg is, or what it means that a birder was allowed there during the war. The man across from me is still shaking his head, as though he is engaged in a permanent quarrel with history; the twins carry on with their whispered consultation. I look at the box and feel like a fool. I had expected to find a membership card of the Dutch fascists, hard evidence of collaboration, testimonials by surviving Engelandvaarders—not a memo about pigeons.

At the bottom of the report is a brief addendum: the suspect has died as the result of a bomb attack. Attached to this

I find a second document from the political investigative unit dated May 2, 1947, in scrawled handwriting: "In my opinion, abetting the enemy, catching pigeons in the *binnenhof*, is not of a sufficiently serious nature (if proven) to justify posthumous charges."

No Engelandvaarders. No smoking gun. Irritated, I shuffle the papers back together; the security man gives me a cautionary look and I secretly dare him to say something, just so I can snap back that this box is incomplete, the archive is incomplete, that they're not doing history much of a favor with this measly stash of scrap paper. But he has already turned his gaze elsewhere.

With a jerk I shove back my chair, pick up my bag, and walk over to the Afghan hound's counter. My irritation grows with every step. Why didn't anyone take the trouble just to write down what happened? Why must I now make do with a couple of barely legible *Ausweises* and a pile of junk from a desk drawer? A bomb exploded, people were killed and men were sent to jail, lives were compromised, and all that's left is this two-bit legend full of holes and cracks.

When I reach the counter, the Afghan hound gives me a questioning look.

"The box is incomplete."

"Not possible."

"Half the story is missing."

"There are no stories in these boxes, only papers."

"But what I read isn't right."

He smiles pityingly.

"We hear that a lot."

I turn and look at the man who was sitting across from me just now. He is still shaking his head. My belly rumbles. The size of a papaya, the weight of a soccer ball, I read this morning. Nine weeks have gone by and still no overall picture. I leave the reading room, go through the hallway and into the foyer. I hesitate at the revolving door. Will I get fined for not clearing up? When I turn to walk back, out of the corner of my eye I spot the head-shaker seated at one of the tables at the deserted coffee bar. He waves, gestures invitingly at the empty table next to him. I look around; we are the only two in this huge echo chamber.

Why not. Take a break, consider my next move. The tables are clustered absurdly close together, as though they are huddling for cover from the vast emptiness around them.

When I put down my bag, the man leans over and extends his hand.

"Herman."

"Marjolijn."

I'm expecting a conversation, a question, a follow-up after this exchange of names, but Herman opens his weathered attaché case, takes out a book, and starts reading. He shakes his head again, but slower than at the white table just now. From close by it looks entirely natural, like he's rocking a baby. I try to guess his age. His face is a fine web of grooves and wrinkles. His medium-length hair has a metallic color, somewhere between black and silver. And yet he has something youthful about him. From my table I can see the title of his book: *Gray Areas: The Netherlands and the Second World War.*

I take out my laptop and read what I've just typed—the pigeons, the fish—the ridiculous pink Post-it above my notes makes it look even more amateurish.

I gesture to the barista, who is leaning, bored, against the coffee machine six feet away.

He shakes his head. "Self-service."

I chuckle, but he's serious.

"There's nobody here!"

He shrugs wearily.

"There never is. Rules are rules."

Herman looks up from his book and asks what I'll have.

"Cappuccino, extra shot, please."

"We call that a doppio," says the barista, who is close enough to overhear.

Herman ambles over to the counter.

"A doppio and a coffee, please."

"What kind of coffee?"

"Regular coffee."

"Americano?"

"The kind I always drink."

"Americano."

Herman turns toward me with a faint smile, as if to apologize for the jerk behind the counter. While the coffee grinder wails, he sits down at my table and asks if I'm on the trail of something yet. He has to raise his voice over the din.

I tell him that what I've found doesn't feel like a trail, more like a game of blindman's bluff. Herman laughs: a clear, wide-open laugh that at once makes him seem like a brash teenager. "You've just started, if I'm not mistaken," he says.

I feel like I've been caught out. Has he already figured out, after such a short time at that table, that I've never been in an archive before? Am I making beginner's blunders?

"I've been at that table every day for a year," he says. "I know all the faces. This is your first time."

I ask what he's spent a year looking for.

"My father."

"Is his dossier that big?"

Herman hesitates, and I suddenly realize what those pink Post-its are meant for. Not to protect the privacy of the deceased, but of the survivors.

"Sorry," I say. "You don't have to—"

But Herman shakes his head.

"It's not a secret, not anymore. After the war my father was suspected of collaboration. When it got brought to trial, he committed suicide. I was born five months later. The dossier only took me a few hours to read, but I'm afraid it'll take a lifetime to understand."

He takes a small carton of orange juice out of his jacket pocket, carefully pokes the straw through the small foil dot, and continues: "I try to sit there at that white table as someone who lived back then, without the ballast of seventy years' worth of history lessons. That's the only way to approach it. The hard part is to accept that history is made up of people from now, only a different now, that they thought the way we do, they did their best, that their life was one of difficult decisions, genuine suffering, real pain. That it was real and just as messy and chaotic as ours now."

Herman sighs. "It takes time. Lots of time."

I point to my belly, which sticks out visibly in my tight T-shirt.

"I'd like to wrap this up before the baby arrives. I don't have time to sit here for a year sifting through dusty boxes."

I only realize too late how unkind that sounds. But Herman doesn't seem to be offended.

"I don't have much to do," he says matter-of-factly. "I'm

divorced, retired, don't have many friends, and my only child lives in Canada."

How am I supposed to respond to this sad summary of his life?

Fortunately the barista shouts, louder than necessary, that the coffee is ready.

Herman saunters over to the bar. I glance over at his book, which lies open on his table. One sentence catches my eye: "First there was the war, and then there was the story of the war."

Herman returns with our coffee, sets it on the wobbly table, and sits back down. He sees me eyeing his book. "There's a lot of good stuff in it," he says, "but that title is nonsense. The notion that everyone is half good, half bad—that says more about the way we look at things now than about mankind in general. Believing in gray areas *back then* means believing in gray areas *now*."

I say I think it's a nice idea, and again he laughs that buoyant, boyish laugh.

"Do you remember those historical prints we used to have back in grade school?"

I shake my head.

"Illustrations of the Ice Age, the Bronze Age, the Romans, the Middle Ages. I could spend hours looking at them. The figures were so beautifully drawn, they looked so much like us. History felt really close. Tangible. That Neanderthal could have been my neighbor. Much later I learned that the guy who drew them always used himself and people around him as models. So all those ancient and prehistoric figures were really what he saw in the mirror every day. We pretend we want to study and understand the past, but in the end, we look mostly at ourselves."

Herman inquires about my dossier. Before I know it—a fraction of a second—it has happened: I've chosen the myth; well, I wouldn't even call it a choice, it's a reflex, an old habit.

I hear myself tell him about the rascal uncle, the bomblet, the collaborator, the heroic deed, my son's name. As though I had not opened that cardboard box just now, had not read that the traitor maybe wasn't a traitor after all, and maybe everything was different than I'd always believed.

For the first time, I'm aware of the rhythm and the melody of the story. I quickly, superficially, slip the word "bomblet" by, while the word "collaborator" gets drawn out with a sneer. And I know for sure that I always tell it this way, exactly the way I always heard it, as though it's not a story but a song anchored on music staves, an old melody whose sound is more important than its lyrics.

Herman's rapt attention makes me uncomfortable. Is it sincere, or does he hear what I hear? If so, he doesn't show it.

I extend my hand, the way I always do after performing my hero number, but this time it looks as if the hand belongs to someone else, it's swollen and covered in red bug bites. Herman brings the finger with the ring right up under his nose, takes his reading glasses from his breast pocket, and studies the stone. For the first time I'm aware how unwieldy the ring is.

"Family crest?" Herman points to the carving in the stone: three royal eagles, their beaks wide open. I nod, suddenly ashamed of these aggressive raptors that sealed the letters and documents of my family these past couple of centuries.

"Big, isn't it."

"It's a man's ring, I have to wear it on my middle finger."

"How old is it?"

"I guess a little more than a hundred years."

"That's amazing," Herman says. "Two world wars, a century of history, and no more than a few tiny scratches."

I pull back my hand, inspect the unblemished gold that has been pinching my finger this last week because of the buildup of fluids. I imagine it remaining shiny for the rest of my life, while my hand swells, shrinks, ages. It makes me sad. Gold's unfair advantage over skin.

Herman says that I'll start to recognize faces at the white table if I come here regularly. "Those twins, for instance, are trying to figure out why their mother was found floating dead in the Maas at the end of 1945. The police report called it a liquidation. There had been rumors that their mother was a collaborator. She'd had close contact with several German officers, but according to the daughters this was a decoy, and she was actually in the Resistance. They've spent years looking for proof."

I wait for more, but Herman has fallen silent. He stares, lost in thought, out into the empty foyer, alternately sipping coffee and orange juice. Just when I think he's forgotten me, he springs back into action. "Let's go," he says. "The dead await us."

I say I'm only going back to pack up the box.

"Finished already?" Herman asks, surprised.

"It's not what I was looking for."

He smiles kindly, or perhaps solicitously, opens his mouth as though he's going to say something, and then closes it again. His meddling is starting to get on my nerves. My body feels heavier than ever. I want to go home, to bed.

We return to the reading room, past two deserted counters

and the Afghan hound, to the white table. Herman's back is already hunched, as though assuming the posture in advance before delving back into that same dossier about his father.

The folder is exactly where I left it, with the papers in a sloppy pile alongside it. I hastily scoop everything together, already trying to recall the train timetables to Amsterdam. I can't wait until I'm home and can finally pull the covers up over my head. But as I'm about to replace the folder, I see that there's a second one at the bottom of the box. How did I manage to miss it the first time around? I feel my cheeks flush. I've let my impatience get the better of me in front of all of them: Herman, the Afghan hound, the security guy whom I had wanted to snap at earlier, everyone who is sitting so professionally and purposefully around the table. I slowly open the folder. It contains three loose sheets of paper. On the first, at the upper right, is a date: 10 December 1946. And below that: "Report, drawn up and signed by Dr. R. R. Rochat, anatomic pathologist and Dr. P. M. Bakker, head of the anatomic pathology laboratory at the municipal hospital on the Zuidwal."

It is the report of the autopsy performed on the three victims of the bombing. Three lists.

François Boer (52 years old)

1. bones in the left hand crushed
2. multiple injuries on the front of the body
3. several holes in the pericardium and myocardium
4. approximately one liter of blood in the left chest cavity
5. various injuries to the left lung

6. four broken costal cartilages on the left side
7. various holes in the small intestine, the omentum, and the mesothelium
8. injuries to the liver
9. partial tearing of both testicles
10. injuries to the left femoral artery and the aorta
11. two perforations in the wall of the pharynx

Injuries were caused by shards of metal propelled with great force; these were direct and fatal.

Greetje Boer-van Dijk (50 years old)

1. multiple wounds on the front of the body
2. perforation of the abdomen in three places
3. two large tears in the stomach wall
4. one large tear in the liver
5. a hole in the small intestine
6. a hole in the omentum
7. blood and digestive tract contents in the abdominal cavity

Injuries were caused by shards of metal propelled with great force; three of these shards penetrated the abdominal wall.

Jacoba Visser (17 years old)

1. a hole in the small intestine
2. general infection of the peritoneum

3. various injuries to the front of the body, the
   mutilation of the left eye and burn wounds on the face
   and arms.

Injuries were caused by shards of metal propelled with great force; one of these penetrated the abdominal wall and perforated the small intestine; infection of the peritoneum was the cause of death.

On the second page is a statement confirming that François's eldest son identified the bodies. The son was not at the house at the time the bombs exploded. His wife, Maria Johanna, was present, and her sloppily typed statement reads as follows:

The Hague, 5 December 1946.

We were all sitting in the living room. My mother-in-law Greetje sang songs for my son, and I accompanied her on the piano. My father-in-law lit the heating stove and Jacoba set the table.

We heard the motorcycle approach; there was no other street traffic. We heard the motorcycle stop in front of the house and ask something of a passerby. Then the doorbell rang and we heard someone shout, "From Saint Nick! From Saint Nick!" Greetje went downstairs with my son. They came back up with a packet and said, "We didn't see who it was." No one was suspicious; it was December 5th, after all, everyone expects surprises. Greetje handed the packet to François and we gathered around him, curious. He tore off the paper and opened the lid. That's all I can remember.

Underneath her statement was the rest of the story, which Maria Johanna could not or did not want to remember.

The daughter-in-law ran to the back of her house with her baby, where she jumped out of the window. She landed, slightly injured, in the downstairs neighbors' backyard.

Boer was killed instantly. After the explosion his wife staggered to the bedroom doorway, where she bled to death.

Housemaid Jacoba Visser was hit by shrapnel on the front of her body. She dragged herself to the stairs, where she was found. She died three days later of her injuries.

Appalled, I retype the three pages. I am sick to my stomach and taste the bitterness on my tongue that I remember from the first weeks of pregnancy. Saliva fills my mouth. I'm afraid I'll throw up. I try to focus and breathe calmly. It helps, the nausea recedes. But the bad taste remains.

I try to gesture to Herman that I'm leaving, but he is already concentrating on his own history, his head bobbing again. I place the folders back in the cardboard box, more carefully now, all the pages in the right order. In the back of my mind is the absurd thought that I mustn't leave any trail behind, as if that might be able to undo what I've seen. I quickly slip out of the reading room: outdoors, fresh air.

On the train, the lists of injuries keep thumping through my head. Torn liver, perforated stomach wall, crushed hand. Mindful of Herman's words, I try to imagine what it was like that evening. Not the way I usually picture it—in black-and-white, and with a well-ordered story line—but with real shrapnel tearing through real flesh; warm, sticky blood; choking smoke; the screaming, gasping, wailing of dying people; Jacoba fighting for her life on the stairs; hysterical shrieks of Maria Johanna's baby as he plummets in his mother's arms into the backyard. I swallow, but the bitter taste won't go away. Until I saw that list, I could convince myself that the other two victims were probably collaborators too—*boontjes* getting their *loontje*—or else it was, like D said, collateral damage. But now they have names, ages, mangled bodies. They were simply in the wrong place at the wrong time, and I don't know where to draw them in on the map. Perhaps everything is different than I thought, and the reassuring story I grew up with no more than a mishmash of skewed facts.

The list of injuries has the effect of a blizzard. The points of reference I had collected these last weeks vanish under a heavy, white chill. I'm back at square one. A frigid expanse.

Maybe I should call it quits, right here and now. Send the ring to Nelly, finally concentrate on the work that's piling up, find a nice name on one of the millions of baby websites—Zane, Zach, Zeke—and then quietly slip into maternity leave.

Bommenneef was no hero, he was a murderer, and you don't name your son after a murderer. End of story. But what about the liver, the stomach, the burn wounds? The names whispered out of the dossier? They were first murdered, then hushed up. I reach for my phone. I want to call someone, everyone, who has supported me in my Bommenneef bubble these past weeks. I want to read them the list, make sure Jacoba's maimed eye is given its rightful place in the narrative so that there's at least some justice to this story.

I look outside. Hoofddorp. Even in midsummer the gray office blocks resemble a prison complex. Did Frans think about the victims during his time in jail? Did Jacoba's ghost waft through the bars on his window at night?

Jacoba. It's her death that bothers me the most.

Because she put up such a fight.

Because she was the youngest. Seventeen. A child.

Because she might still have been alive today. What a crazy idea. She would be eighty-seven. A woman with a whole life behind her, instead of having evaporated into history during that cold, wet week in December at age seventeen. And here's me having spent twenty-five years bragging about the man who was responsible for it. Again I feel myself blush, my heart race, an angry fist pound my chest. How could I have been so naïve? Even if I wanted to, I can't throw in the towel now. If I don't find out what really happened that night, no one will. The myth will remain intact, and Jacoba invisible. I cannot do what people have been doing for seventy years: leave out the parts they don't like. This story is the first thing I've promised my son. What am I supposed to say when he asks me about the ring? About the certificate? About the name I had in mind for him? *Sorry, I broke my very first promise to you before you were even born, because the truth put me off*? It seems to me a bad start: half a story, a box of traffic fines, and a list of injuries. No way.

And what if Frans didn't know there were others in the house besides François Boer? What if it's true after all that Boer turned twelve Dutch escapees over to the Nazis? The fact that it wasn't proven does not mean it didn't happen. Does it matter? In my confined, sheltered reality, murder is murder. But this didn't happen in my peaceful microcosm, it happened in the aftermath of a devastating war.

Aside from noble motives—justice for the victims, keeping my promise to my son—I know of another reason not to stop. And, to be honest, it's the most pressing. To quit now would be to lose Bommenneef forever. Now that his myth is crumbling, there's nothing left to carry him through time. For a name to survive, it has to be embedded in a story. A word won't stand the test of time on its own. There has to be context. Form. A song with a beginning, a middle, and an end. This is the only insurance against oblivion.

Hoofddorp recedes into the distance and we cross the A4, the road Bommenneef took to Brussels back in 1946 to fetch his sweetheart Nelly. I feel the angry fist in my chest relax, the bitter taste in my mouth slowly melt away.

If I don't want to lose my hero, I need a new story. The true story.

And so, two days later, I reluctantly make my way back to B's small apartment in The Hague.

17 WEEKS LEFT

WALKING FROM THE bus station to B's apartment, I notice for the first time that the streets in her neighborhood are named after fallen heroes of the Resistance. On one of the public squares is a monument "To Those Who Died for the Fatherland." A small sign says: Adopted by the Students of "The Ark" Primary School. An accompanying photograph shows a group of children standing in front of the monument, their arms laden with flowers.

I think back on what Frans asked Nelly: How long does a war last? Nelly's answer—"until peace comes"—indeed misses the mark.

I got off to a slow start this morning. I spent the whole night carrying out electrocutions. Two days ago D hung up a mosquito net, but the bugs outsmarted us and found their way into the net anyway. What should have been a safe haven turned out to be a snare. The net is gone, the electro-rackets have returned. And the house once again stinks of charred insects.

B takes her time answering the door. I resolve to get straight to the point this time, and not waste half a day again on superficial chitchat. I want to hear from her if Frans was the kind of man who would sacrifice innocent lives for his ideals, whether he'd have still ordered the bombing if he had known there were people there who had nothing to do with the evil he was out to avenge. B knew him for half his life, she ironed his neckties, washed his hair, called him every week. She should know what he was capable of.

When she finally opens the door, she eyes me suspiciously.

"Well, if it isn't Agatha Christie."

She answers my smile with a dirty look. She's obviously not amused by my digging around in newspapers and government archives.

B's rigid body is packed into a light-gray suit. She sits upright in the chair like a radio antenna, the glistening knot in her hair a silver transmitter. She pours me a halfhearted cup of tea and asks what's wrong with my eye.

"Mosquitoes," I reply, as I place my hand on the lump. The skin is warm, my blood throbs under the swelling. An allergic reaction to the bite, or perhaps just fatigue; even after hours of electrocution, the maddening buzz kept me awake. Last night I was sure that one of the mosquitoes had laid her eggs in my ear, that I myself had become a breeding ground. The buzzing seemed to be coming from within me, from somewhere behind my eardrum. I looked it up, dead tired at my laptop, but read that only an extremely rare species of tropical insect uses the human ear as a repository for its progeny.

"Before you go telling me all kinds of things about Frans," B says, "I just want to make it clear that it won't change my opinion of him, ever. I knew him. I know who he was."

Her voice seems thinner than the last time, and the words sound reedy and high-pitched.

I nod. "That's why I'm here. You knew him. If Frans had known there were innocent people at home, if he had known that François Boer wasn't a proven collaborator, would he have still had the bomb delivered?"

All she has to do is shake her head. A simple no would suffice to keep our hero intact. A careless, sloppy hero, maybe, but nonetheless a man who was true to his ideals. B's eyes are still glued to the swollen half of my face. "Have you ever had the feeling that everything you believed in was slipping away?" she asks. "That life was turned upside down, and you had to hold tight to keep from losing control altogether? That's how it was in 1946. Those newsreels of flags and festivities were just part of the story. The other part was chaos. Total chaos. It was as though everyone had lost the war, including—especially—the *good guys.*" Again, that exaggerated British accent.

I take a sip of tea in an attempt to stall for time. I'm afraid I already know what her next question will be. The question that World War II has saddled us with for good, the question asked every Memorial Day, every Liberation Day, in every history lesson at school, as though answering it can shield us from the next catastrophe: "What would *you* do?"

I shrug. B looks at me intensely and repeats the question. "If everything you always believed in slipped through your fingers, what would you do?"

Would I deliver a bomb to a house where children were present? Sacrifice another life for the sake of my own convictions?

No.

Unless . . .

It depends on your definition of life. And of sacrifice. The pregnancy I broke off after eight weeks felt like a sacrifice, not so much on account of a specific conviction—or maybe yes, after all: the conviction that my life was not one where a twenty-one-year-old gets pregnant by a Rotterdam bartender; the conviction that my life was about to take a sudden, very wrong turn. So I made an about-face. It was the first time I felt that if life did not conform to my self-image, then I would adjust life and leave my self-image intact. The first time I experienced the devastating potential of expectations.

You can't compare an abortion to a bomb attack, but it's the only blood sacrifice I can come up with on short notice. Only thing is, it doesn't seem a befitting response in this decent little apartment.

My stomach rumbles. I don't know if it's me or the baby, or maybe a hungry baby—does our hunger coincide? The hole in Jacoba's intestine flashes through my mind. Her maimed eye. B notices my discomfort and changes her tone. "Apple pie," she says, quite a bit friendlier now, and goes into the kitchen. Keep questioning her. Don't be satisfied with her half answers and useless anecdotes.

"What do you think drove Frans to do it?" I ask B when she returns with the plates. She slowly walks to the table, more measured than necessary, sets them down in slow motion, and then shuffles back to her chair. She leans back and heaves a deep sigh.

"Where to start? Frans always wanted to be a hero, I think. He'd always been a loner. He never really got over his mother's death. In some ways he stayed a lonely little boy. Someone who wanted to be noticed and admired, even though he would never admit it."

As I eat her oversweet apple pie, B talks about Frans's solitude, his yearning for the affection and security he had missed as a child. She tells of his strong sense of justice, his drive, his humor. I feel myself settle back into the old, comfy song whose lyrics I know by heart. The tidy, wrinkle-free myth, *boontje* and his *loontje*. The belief that his intentions were honest, that he couldn't possibly have known there were innocents in harm's way and that François might not have been the devil he took him for.

"Frans was an old-fashioned hero," B says. "He didn't waste words on what had to be done, he just did it. There's so much *talk* these days, so much agonizing over the pros and cons. All it does is sow doubt. Frans never had doubts."

"Not even when he heard there were other victims?"

"Probably not. He knew he was in the right. Not just anybody gets a certificate from Montgomery." She says that last bit with such certainty that I don't dare ask any further.

On the way to the kitchen for fresh tea she lays five red-painted nails on my shoulder.

"Maybe he not only missed having a mother, but a child too."

"I know. That's why I got the ring."

"No, not in a general sense. I mean a specific child. There were rumors about a baby with his first wife. That she couldn't find a wedding dress big enough to conceal it." I think of Nelly's story about the mumps that made Frans infertile. But maybe that was only later.

"If there had been a child, why did he send the ring to my grandmother? And why haven't I ever heard anything about it?"

"They say it was a son who died right after it was born."

The combination of the words "dead" and "son" gives me a jolt.

Before I can say anything, she shakes her head and says, "I don't know anything. I'm just repeating what was whispered."

"A dead mother. A dead son. A war," I sum up. "I'd call those extenuating circumstances."

B throws her long arms in the air. "What else is life but a series of extenuating circumstances?"

16 WEEKS LEFT

FRANS LIGHTS HIS last cigarette, inhales deeply, and considers that he could just as well have left it in the pack: the corridor of the maternity ward is already dizzyingly thick with smoke. After all, what else do the men have to do than inhale and exhale tobacco smoke and pace in silence?

The yuletide decorations on the walls are the worse for wear, the paint chipping off the angels and stars. From the ward comes the cries of babies and mothers. Occasionally a door opens to this din, a man gets called in; the ones left behind watch him with a combination of envy and pity.

His cigarettes finished, Frans strolls down the Herengracht. The water is as black as the sky. The city is like a ghost town.

How long does childbirth take?

Maybe he's already a father by the time he reaches the next bridge; in the space of one footstep he's been moved up a generation. He always thought the transformation from son to father would be marked by some spectacle—a ceremony, a cloudburst, at least a flash of lightning—but in fact you just sit around and wait, and everything changes except yourself.

At the bridge he suddenly knows for sure: the child, his child, has been born. He turns back.

Does he hope for a son, a daughter? What he hopes for is warmth. For something to hold on to that he'll never have to let go of.

He rushes through the entrance, up the stairs, to the ward. From Carolina's room comes a muffled whimpering. A nurse stands in the doorway—in the semidarkness she looks like a heavyset white angel. She beckons him, her face somber. He looks into the corridor, tries to make eye contact with his fellow fathers-to-be, but they have turned away.

His heart skips a beat. Something's wrong. He hesitates, but now the angel addresses him. "Sir, your wife needs you."

She leads him into the room. Carolina is as white as a sheet, her eyes are closed. *Your wife. My wife.* It sounds much too intimate for someone he has known so briefly. He would never have married her if she hadn't gotten pregnant that one night. For two months now, he wakes up startled every morning alongside that strange, oversized body. He tries to look into Carolina's eyes, but she keeps them shut. There is nothing between them except the child in the white wooden cradle next to her bed. He hears it whimper, a soft, lamenting sound. It does not bode well: he had expected vehement, vital cries. The nurse nudges him toward the baby.

He resists. His legs are weak, he can barely budge, but the hefty angel is firm. "Your son," she says. He repeats the words to himself. *My son.* It sounds softer, easier than *my wife.*

The son is a wrinkly, purple baby, half hidden under a woolen blanket. His head is as round as a full moon and seems too big for the wispy little neck it is attached to. One arm is lying on top of the blanket; it's so thin he doesn't dare touch it. The fingers clasping the blanket are like tiny blue claws.

"My son." He had imagined him chubby and rosy-cheeked. A burly thing with a booming voice, not this anemic little bird.

The angel is standing on the other side of the crib.

When he looks at her, she shakes her head. Carolina still has not yet opened her eyes. He cautiously wriggles his pinky into the fragile little hand, feels the smooth, cold fingers on his skin.

Everything about his son reeks of deficiency. He is too skinny, too purple, too quiet. Frans cannot give him what he needs. Kilos, color, voice. He just stands there, with his pinky in the crib and a head full of darkness.

A name, he thinks, all I can give him is a name.

The name that had been waiting for him since before his birth: his name, his father's name, his father's father's name. He says it out loud in the otherwise noiseless room, half expecting that the skies will clear and fate will be reversed. But all remains still in that terrible darkness.

How long does Frans stand bent over the crib with those weightless hands in his? Years, centuries, half a second. He feels the skin gradually go cold, the tiny arm blue, the face ashen. A black ebb tide sucks his son deathward. The little fingers sink back into the crib, the birdlike chest stops moving. He looks at his son's eyelids, two soft, white almonds in an expression of infinite sadness. "He is dead," the nurse says, but Frans doesn't hear her. There is a thick pane of frosted glass between his head and the world.

———

No, this isn't working. I'm trying to write myself a way into the brain of a little boy who has lost his mother, of a resentful adolescent raised in a loveless environment, of a man who has lost his son. In my fictionalized world, Frans always gets the short end of the stick: with his father, his social class, world politics—but Jacoba's maimed eye keeps drawing me back to the facts. December 5, 1946. An explosion, three deaths. It really did happen. You can't go inventing things around this.

And yet I do. Invent. Or should I say: devise. B, for instance, does not live in the neighborhood named after Resistance heroes; she lives alongside it. My friend does not rent an atelier in Frans's garrison. She does rent an atelier, and the base where Frans once served is now an artists' colony, so it could have been. But it wasn't. I shift things around, invent a show-and-tell presentation. Not for the standing ovation and the best marks in the class, but because otherwise it doesn't tally. Because I need roads to connect the various regions that are starting to appear on the map. But now I've spent days wandering aimlessly among extenuating circumstances, in the fiction of a new myth: Bommenneef and the dead son.

I don't know if Frans Jr. existed. And if he did, I don't know what he died of, or if Frans Sr. was there when it happened.

I don't even know what a dying baby looks like. I picture the dead baby in W. F. Hermans's *The Darkroom of Damocles*. With eyes closed in "an expression of infinite sadness," which the father stared at "as if a thick pane of frosted glass were being held before his eyes."

I SEARCH THE BOX Aunt S gave me for hints of a child. The divorce papers give Frans and Carolina's wedding date as October 16, 1936. He was twenty-seven, she a year older. If B was right, if the marriage took place shortly before she gave birth, then it was most likely, in those days, a hasty, hush-hush event. Formalities at city hall, drinks with some friends, and then off to the brand-new house in Nieuwer-Amstel—now the suburb of Amstelveen—to the address on the divorce certificate and on various letters in the cardboard box.

A few days later I have an appointment in that part of town, so I cycle past the house.

It is still there. A sturdy, red specimen in an impeccable

neighborhood, the picture of decency. Space, light, backyards full of well-brought-up children. The perfect place to raise a family. Behind the picture window alongside the front door, a woman sits at the table; next to her, a toddler is hunched over a drawing pad. Between them is a large teapot on one of those warmers with a small candle underneath. It is the kind of house you'll feel nostalgic for later, that you'll remember as a place where there was always a pot of tea on the table, kept warm above a little tea light. The toddler points to something on the paper, the woman smiles and kisses the child's forehead.

I consider ringing the bell, but what for? Frans and Carolina only lived here for a short time. The marriage fell apart and Frans, according to the divorce papers, moved to the city center. What if Carolina and Frans had raised a son in this house? Would Frans's life have taken a different path? Would he have ever become Bommenneef?

Back home, I phone all the cemeteries in that neighborhood, but nowhere is there a baby's grave from 1936.

I ask my father, a retired pediatrician, if he knows what happened in those days to babies that died at birth.

Until the 1980s, he says, it was assumed the parents had no emotional bond with a stillborn child or one that died soon after birth. "They were often whisked away. You were supposed to forget about it as quickly as possible. The babies were usually cremated."

"And the ashes?"

"They got scattered somewhere near the hospital."

I think back on that morning in the abortion clinic, installed in a large, cold chair with my legs spread and my gaze fixed on the world map on the wall. I had opted for a local anesthetic; I wanted to be present, not let myself dodge the reality of this blunder.

The doctor, a small, thin woman, placed a hand on my arm and pointed to the world map. "It's going to hurt for a moment. Just focus on which countries you'd like to visit."

On the table next to me was a suction pump with a flexible tube attached.

Somalia, I thought. Uzbekistan. Chile.

As she inserted the tube, I did my very best not to think of the being that was growing unawares inside me, getting bigger by the second, forming a skeleton this week. "I'll count to three," the doctor said. Greenland. Russia. Canada. A gurgling sound, everything in my body resisted, would not let go of that small unwanted life. A sharp pain flashed somewhere in my abdomen—so there's my womb, I thought.

She removed the tube from my body, leaving behind a stinging, tingling emptiness.

I asked if I could see it. She hesitated. "There's nothing to see."

I very much wanted to see that nothing.

She reluctantly held up a gray cardboard container, filled to the brim with thick, dark blood with flecks floating in it.

"Are those limbs?"

She shook her head.

"There's nothing left."

She was uncomfortable, I could tell, with my look, my questions, but I couldn't do otherwise. I had to look, keep looking, at that pulverized prospect of life.

"And now?"

"Now we rinse it down the drain," she said quietly.

She slowly walked over to the stainless steel sink in the corner of the surgery, turned on the faucet, and ever so carefully, almost lovingly (I hoped), let the blood and the blobs swirl into the drain along with the water.

An hour later, I stumbled outside. From the zoo across the street, an elephant stared at me. The enormous beast stood a few meters from the rush of traffic, its heavy head leaning against the fence of its habitat. I imagined the remains of that cardboard container ending up in the groundwater, permeating the moat surrounding her terrain.

"Soon you'll drink my baby," I whispered.

She moved her trunk back and forth over the fence, as though trying to caress me from a distance, as if she knew why I was standing there crying.

I cannot find a grave for Frans Jr., but I do come across a death notice in the archive of the Catholic daily *De Tijd*. It's no more than half a line long. "Frans Julian Johan van Heemstra," and after that: "1 d." One day. He's listed in between Marie, who died at eight months, and Lena, five months. He was born and died on November 26, 1936. I'm surprised at how hard that half a line hits me. Such a long name for such a short life. How much of the world do you experience if you only live for one day? The violence of your birth, some vague specks of light and dark, maybe some milk, a warm washcloth. A smaller universe is hard to imagine.

I wonder if my grandmother knew about Frans Jr. The fact

that he existed adds weight to my promise to her. Frans was not just hoping for a namesake he could give the ring to. He was looking for a stand-in for that little boy who should have been given his only piece of jewelry. It was a last-ditch effort to get things to line up in his otherwise messy life.

14 WEEKS LEFT

IT'S STRANGE WHAT this counting down does to the weeks. They become their own little era, each with its own characteristics and constructs. Week 26 is the week of wild dreams and short nights. I am in a constant state of drowsiness. New complaints are added to the existing repertoire: a permanent headache, and the feeling that a belt is being pulled tighter and tighter around my midriff. Shortness of breath, seeing stars.

The autumn is warm and humid. To escape the mosquitoes, D and I drive up to the family bungalow in Friesland, a small white farmhouse surrounded by pear trees. D lies in the grass reading, I sit in the shade of the elder tree, staring at the sheep in the adjacent meadow. A few days of "real togetherness," that was the plan, but since we've been here, we are revolving in different orbits. I don't think D is bothered by this. I even suspect that for him, this is the optimal kind of "togetherness": a minimum of conversation, a maximum of relaxation. Not my cup of tea. I should have brought my laptop so I could have continued combing the National Archive's database. I want to read the summary of Frans's court case. I want to know how he defended himself, what he said in the presence of his cohorts and the victims' families.

Now a week has been wasted on sheep and grass, while I could have been in the coolness of the reading room, sitting across from Herman with a cardboard box full of new information. I know it's childish of me, but it feels unfair that D is blithely engrossed in his book while I sit here gasping for breath. I'm struck by the maddening matter-of-factness of it being *my* job, that it's my body that's bloated with fluid and not his, that my organs are getting squashed together to make room for this new life. If this child is as much his as mine, if it's going to get his last name and we're to share all the rights, why am I the only one here who is fat and short of breath?

Why doesn't he ask me how I'm doing every five minutes?

I always thought pregnancy brings a man and woman closer together. That'd be thanks to the overworked image depicted on all those baby websites, in women's magazines, in folders at the gynecologist, on people's mantelpieces: the beaming father-to-be standing behind his pregnant wife with his hands firmly clasped around her belly. The image propagated as a sign of solidarity. Only now do I see its true meaning: the man is hiding behind her, he clamps himself to that big ball of flesh because otherwise he'll be standing there empty-handed.

Aside from the moments when he can briefly share in the experience—an ultrasound, the first visible movement under the taut skin—he has nothing to hold on to. This whole pregnancy thing is the fast track to growing apart. The one swells up to whalelike proportions, becomes oversensitive and weepy; the one is no longer one but two, and has to continually deal with the sci-fi of an alien living inside her, complete with growing pains and sleeplessness, while the other one just stays himself.

I hoist myself out of my chair, loudly clap my hands a few times, startling both D and the sheep. Enough grass for now. "Let's do something," I say.

D gets up slowly, lays a warm hand on my cheek.

"What would you like to do?" Ashamed of what I was just thinking, I take his hand in mine.

"Something together. Go somewhere. For a drive, a walk, it doesn't matter, as long as we move. How about Franeker? The planetarium built by Eise Eisinga, the astronomer."

An hour later we're standing in front of the small brick building. D smiles at the sight of the weathered stone tablet depicting a stork, way at the top of the gable. "Look," he says. "Three hundred years ago a child was born here."

It's quiet inside. "Slow day," says the woman at the ticket counter.

She gives us a folder with a short biography of Eisinga. The first thing that catches my eye is the part about the death of his son Jelte, who was meant to have followed in his father's footsteps. The woman directs us to the annex and the attic. As we slowly make our way down the hall, I read about how Eisinga reconstructed our solar system in his living room. It took him seven years. He had a day job as a wool comber; at night he hammered away at his universe. And soon we're standing directly under a gilded sun.

It's overwhelming. The miniature planets, painted half gold (for daytime) and half black (for night), make their way in real time over tracks in the ceiling: the slowest, Saturn (a perfect wooden sphere!), takes nearly thirty years to make a single revolution. The walls are crowded with dials: a moondial, a sundial, week, day, and hour dials. Everything moves in bigger or smaller circles, in all manner of ways of dividing time. It works; it fits. The unfathomable darkness above us has been reduced to manageable, room-sized proportions. Planets that fit in the palm of your hand, driven by a slow-moving mechanism of gears carved out of oak, which in turn is kept in motion by metal counterweights in an old cupboard.

"It's like a time machine," D whispers, his voice full of wonder. I hear a sentence in my mind: "Listen: Billy Pilgrim has come unstuck in time." Maybe that is what Eisinga wanted, to harness time, to become unstuck like Billy Pilgrim in Kurt Vonnegut's *Slaughterhouse-Five*, a man who traveled back and forth between random moments in the past and the future.

I ask D which moment in time he would most like to travel to. "The near future," he replies. "The first time I fall asleep with my son. That must feel great, spending the whole night alongside a tiny little body, knowing you'll wake up next to each other. And you?"

"December 5, 1946."

"Oh yeah. Of course," D sighs. "Your hero's tale. And which moment, exactly?"

"The moment Bommenneef writes out the hit list."

No, earlier, I think as soon as the words have left my mouth: the moment he formulates the plan. Or earlier, the death of his baby son. Or of his mother. The moment when someone, his future niece, should have been standing next to him with a hand on his shoulder and the right words on her lips.

D interrupts my reverie with a knock on the wooden alcove bed. "You know what this is?"

I shake my head.

"The perfect nursery."

From somewhere above us comes a soft, regular ticking. It is the clock, I read in the folder, that keeps everything in motion. We stand there for a few more minutes, silently gazing up at the planets on the ceiling. I get a lump in my throat. So it *is* possible to ward off chaos. With dedication, with love, with time. I want to impress D with my favorite quote by Immanuel Kant, but pregnancy dementia has gnawed away at my memory. I get no further than "the starry sky above me and the moral law within me" and something with "awe" and "admiration."

Eise Eisinga lost his son, but he had his stars.

Bommenneef lost his son, but he had his moral law.

Only, that moral law did not earn him awe or admiration. A year earlier Frans would probably have been decorated. Instead he got a prison sentence. How long does a war last? Does the war revolve with us, like the earth around the sun? I try to imagine how Frans stood in the courtroom, how he faced the judge. Convinced of the rightness of his deed, not ruffled by collateral fatalities, because a single life is meaningless in the light of the stars and one's own moral law.

13 WEEKS LEFT

WHAT A RELIEF to see the sheep and the lindens disappear in the rearview mirror. No more time to lose. Uneasy about my persistent physical complaints, D insists I call the obstetrician's office from the car. I get their voice mail, which probably means they're in the middle of a delivery. I leave a message that I'm dizzy and seeing stars, and ask if I can move my appointment up.

Back home, I go straight upstairs, sit down at my desk, and flip open the laptop. The National Archive website soon gives me what I'm after: there is a written report of Frans's court case. I send an email asking to see it, and within ten minutes I have an answer: the box will be ready for me today.

On my way to the station, the obstetrician calls back. "I just heard your message. It doesn't sound good. I want to see you right away."

I curse and turn back.

Sitting in the stuffy waiting room, I look with horror at my bare legs. Blue veins wind their way up my calves to my knees. No idea how this riverscape got there. I follow the thick meanders with my finger, try in vain to press them back into my flesh. An archipelago of mosquito bites has formed among the rivers. We had hoped that a week's absence of human blood in our house would have driven them to look for new feeding grounds, but when we got back from Friesland this afternoon, they were sitting there on the walls, waiting for us. With his bag still on his back, D called the pest control. "There's got to be a nest here somewhere," I heard him say, "and we have to get rid of it." I thought: mosquitoes don't build nests. The only nest in the house is me. And I imagined them coming to fumigate *me* with their spray canisters full of poison. The man on the phone promised to come as soon as possible.

In the examination room, the concerned obstetrician listens to the summary of what's ailing me. She winds the blood-pressure sleeve around my left arm, pushes the start button, and watches the counter shoot up, tick back down, and eventually settle on a score: 150/98.

"I was afraid of that," she says. "Far too high. Could be pre-eclampsia. We'll have to do a blood test. The best thing would be to go straight to the hospital, I'll call and let them know you're coming. We don't want to waste any time with this." I phone D, who arrives within five minutes and races to the hospital as if I'm already in labor.

Once inside, he grabs the first available wheelchair. "Here, sit down." I want to resist; I can walk just fine, but D pushes me into the chair and wheels me at top speed toward the elevator. I'm brought to a small white room in the obstetrics ward and made to lie down on a strangely high bed fitted out with all manner of bars, wheels, and handgrips.

A nurse hurries in, takes my blood pressure again, repeats what the obstetrician said: "Too high." A cartful of needles and tubes is pulled up alongside me, I'm jabbed, I pee in a little jar, I answer questions. Then a man comes in, introduces himself as Dr. Dukhi, the duty gynecologist. Everything about Dr. Dukhi is soft: his hands, his voice, his hair that dances in dark locks around his face. He looks at me first before speaking; it is a nice kind of being looked at, like he wants to make human, nonmedical contact before we start in on blood counts and risk factors. Now that he's here, a sense of calm has finally descended over the room. I can breathe again.

"It's hypertension," he says gently.

"Hyper what?" D asks.

"Tension, hypertension," replies Dr. Dukhi. "Pregnancy poisoning, although the term is misleading. It's probably an overactive immune response to the placenta, which holds foreign substances from the father."

"So she's allergic to the baby?" D asks with half a grin.

"To the father's half, at least," Dr. Dukhi replies amiably. He pats D on the shoulder. "Not your fault." I can't tell from his expression whether he's joking or not. He turns back to me and says, "We'll take it from here. We want to keep the baby inside for as long as possible. Your job is to get plenty of rest and come by every other day for a checkup."

I look around the room, my eyes follow the bare walls decorated with the occasional sticker of a large pink flower, peeling
loose around the edges. Every other day: this throws my whole
timetable into disarray.

"You'll have to make some adjustments," Dr. Dukhi says.
He probably noticed my startled look. "But it's for a good
cause." I nod. Of course. A good cause. The cause that is taking over my life, slowly but surely, without sacrificing anything
of itself. The cause I can't quite get a grip on, and for which I
can't prepare myself except to give it a name and a story. Which
requires me to go to The Hague today.

But first a nurse attaches me to a large machine. "We'll measure the fetus's heartbeat and register its movements, and check
the uterine activity," she explains. I nod absently, still taken
aback by Dr. Dukhi's pronouncement. Two straps are attached
around my belly, and we hear the rapid heartbeat of our son,
the gallop of a tiny horse. D looks shaken, and I feel a childish
satisfaction that my body is now also his problem.

For half an hour we listen, hand in hand, to the muffled
white noise.

Looking through the window into the corridor, I see the
birth announcements on the wall: Kees, Mo, Fien, Ajouad,
Marieke, Marijn.

D follows my gaze. "We should also start thinking about the
birth announcement," he says.

I nod.

I once read about a nomadic tribe in Australia whose cus-
tom it is to name the child after the place where the mother
first learned she was pregnant. A forest. A lake. A rock. Like
in the olden days, when foundlings were named after the place

where they were discovered. Perhaps it's more logical to name a child after a place than after a person. A place gives the new life room to grow, whereas a person already occupies that space, suffocating you with his or her past and pratfalls.

We could name the baby after the small park in front of our house, where I finally dared take the pregnancy test out of my bag, half an hour after I peed over it. Or after the slender blossoms I was sitting under when I called D with the news, or after the flock of starlings that took off, screeching, the moment he answered.

D drives me home, installs me on the sofa, and leaves for work. As soon as he shuts the door behind him I get up, take my bag, and cycle to the station. I do my best to move as calmly as possible. No hurry, no stress. I know exactly what D would say if he saw me get onto the train to The Hague right now. I know what everyone would say, but lying in bed brooding isn't doing my blood pressure any good either. No, if there's one place I'm at ease, it's in a warm train that will take me to the dossier I need. The court report of Bommenneef's trial.

When the revolving door spits me out, I spot Herman in the coffee corner with his book open in front of him. This time, instead of orange juice, he's got a minicarton of Fristi, a sweetened milk drink. I watch him as he slowly turns a page. There is something light and dreamy in the way he moves, as though his limbs are almost weightless, as if he's not an almost-elderly man with gray hair and a hunched back.

He looks up and breaks into a big grin when he sees me. I return the smile and slowly make my way over to him. I feel light-headed; with every step, a row of stars dances around my field of vision. He's at the counter ordering me a cappuccino before I've even reached his table. Two minutes later he plonks it down in front of me. "Extra shot. Good to see you again."

I sit down next to him and jab him with my elbow. "Haven't you got that dossier memorized by now?"

He gives me a quizzical look.

Stupid and insensitive of me to start right in about his father. I feel the blood rush to my cheeks.

"The dossier," I stammer. "Isn't that the same one as before?"

Herman laughs. "What kind of old fool do you take me for?"

My cheeks burn.

"So what have you spent a whole year reading?"

"I'm following the threads."

"Threads?"

"It's a web. My father's dossier leads to the dossiers of the men he betrayed, and their dossiers in turn lead to other ones. This way I'm exploring all the stories surrounding my father's."

"How many stories are thrashing around in your web, then?"

Herman thinks for a moment. "About 450, I think. Of victims, perpetrators, a little bit of everything."

Herman sips his coffee, and then some Fristi, and chuckles at my surprise.

"With every new dossier," he begins hesitantly, "I move farther away from my father, and yet it still feels like I'm getting closer to him. For a long time I thought I had to figure *him* out, but more and more I'm realizing that a person is part of a web, and understanding that web and its structure is the only way to really get to know the person."

"But isn't that a roundabout method? There will be people in that web who have nothing to do with your father."

He nods. "Maybe it's that unknown factor that I'm looking for. I might be reading the dossier of a perfect stranger whose story is only obliquely related to my father's, and suddenly something will click."

"Don't you lose track of cause and effect?"

"You can't tell these stories chronologically. They need to be approached differently to get the complete picture."

"But that doesn't do justice to what happened."

"A story doesn't do justice to the dead anyway. In fact, it shortchanges them."

Herman stirs his coffee. The barista thumbs through a magazine. Outside, commuters rush to and from the station. Out there, the present moves toward the future. Here inside, all there is is space and coffee, a barista of few words, and two people in search of completeness. The foyer is a hinge in time. The revolving door is still, the counters are unstaffed. Beyond the barrier gates farther up, in the coolness of the reading room, are the boxes full of history.

Herman asks me the name of the man whom Bommenneef blew up. "François," I reply. "François Boer."

He repeats the name, as though to learn it by heart, which gives me an uneasy feeling. Then he leaps up out of his chair. "The dead await us." As we head to the reading room, I notice how strangely he walks. There's no regularity in his gait; he takes big steps, then small ones. He's marching out of step— but out of step with what? With the way things tally.

The dead who await me today are the ones who killed last time's dead. Those said to have been on the "right" side of history, who left behind commendations, medals, and names that will be passed from generation to generation. The heroes of the Resistance, the Bommenneefs.

Today the Afghan hound is wearing a gold choker around his skinny neck. When he slides the box across the counter, I notice how long and dirty his fingernails are. This dossier has not come from the Extraordinary Jurisdiction archives. Accordingly, I'm allowed to sit wherever I want, but I still gravitate toward the big white table, I think out of some guilty conscience, but in regard to whom, I can't say. As before, there is just one chair free, my chair. In addition to Herman, across from me, and the twins next to him, I recognize a few other faces.

The box contains a well-thumbed folder that I presume was once red but is now a faded orangey color. At the upper right, in scrawled handwriting, is a brief description of the contents. *Report of hearing regarding bomb attack on 5 December 1946.*

The report is five pages long, although "page" is a rather big word for the yellowed sheets covered in stains and smears (there's even an edge burned off one of them—the cigarette of a duty detective? An attempt to destroy evidence?). I carefully place them side by side on the table, open the Facts folder on my laptop, and begin typing.

The report begins with the plea by Frans's lawyer, Ponte. He appeals to the court's empathy: "Whoever wishes to understand my client must understand that he is a man of his time. One cannot understand the man without understanding his time; cannot understand his time without understanding his war; this case goes beyond the question of the guilt of a single person; this case is about us all, the entire postwar society."

"Nonsense," snarls a voice under her breath from across the table. It's one of the twins. The other is glaring angrily at the sheet of paper lying in front of her. Their whispering has turned into a hissing is-so-is-not that gradually envelops the table. People glance up, clear their throat, shoot them dirty looks. Only Herman stays engrossed in his dossier. The sister who started the palaver scuffs her chair back and marches out of the reading room. Quiet returns. I reread what I've just typed and try to imagine Ponte speaking these words. Finger raised, stately posture, voice at full volume. I wonder if his listeners were receptive to his argument. I am, at least. Probably because of that rhetorical repetition of the word "understand."

You cannot understand a man without understanding his war. Do I understand Bommenneef's war? What do I know about it? A hand minus a thumb is my first and most vivid association. Specifically, the hand belonging to Mrs. Koopmans, who used to clean for us. "Chopped off by the Krauts," she replied when, after years of sneaking looks at it, I mustered up the courage to ask. The Nazis were after her brother—a wanted Resistance figure—and tried to coerce his hiding place out of her, but Mrs. Koopmans refused. She considered it a fair deal, a thumb in return for a life. She let me touch it, that dimple in her old hand. Under the soft skin was an unseen stump, it felt hard and rough, made me think of the base of a chopped-down tree.

Ponte continues his plea with an accusation against Corporal De Boer. "My client, who contributed substantially to the Resistance, was drawn into this scheme by his subordinate Ate

Tekele De Boer. Witnesses confirm that the captain changed after De Boer was assigned to his regiment, a man with a reputation as a loose cannon and who had been involved in racketeering during the Hunger Winter of '44–'45."

I quickly retype this as I read, shortening a word here and there, curious where it's all headed. Maybe this is what B meant when she said Frans had been "duped into it." Maybe it wasn't Captain van Heemstra after all, but Corporal De Boer who had masterminded the attack, and that Frans had been dragged into a sinister plot cooked up by another. Another new twist in the story: Bommenneef the fall guy.

But right underneath Ponte's accusation, De Boer's counsel claims just the opposite. It was Captain van Heemstra who had manipulated the corporal. He calls Frans an "untrustworthy fellow" and says there had been rumors about him, as head of the motor vehicle facility, running an auto-parts smuggling operation from France. His team is said to have also made off with some eighty vehicles and a large number of tires. The men felt that their role in the Resistance justified earning a little extra cash on the side. Captain van Heemstra, says the lawyer, was an "egocentric automobile fanatic" who was a master in exploiting his subordinates. "My client wanted to do the right thing, as he had always done, and assumed that Van Heemstra was leading him along an enlightened path."

I bring the yellowed paper right up to my nose, study the sloppy typography, as though the letters themselves will reveal which of the two opposing stories on the page is true. It smells like moss, or no, like basement: dampness and stale air. Frans the victim or Frans the culprit: I find both choices equally unappealing.

The next page starts by stating that following his account, De Boer's lawyer reads a poem "that his client, in deepest despair, wrote while in detention." The poem follows:

And now I humbly beg your honor,
Relieve me of this cross of shame,
I cannot bear it any longer,
for it has ruined my good name.

I read and reread the lines. So this is where De Boer ended up: no *boontje* and *loontje* but shame and name. The childish rhyme irritates me. I've already chosen sides in this case, and as far as I'm concerned, De Boer is brazenly playing the court. He hopes that with a cheap ditty he'll be able to manipulate the following rhyme word: "blame."

I skim further, hoping for some sign of remorse from Frans, preferably more eloquent than the corporal's. But all I see are brief witness statements from fellow military men, none of whom appears to be well-disposed to Frans. "The captain operated as though the whole world were his enemy," says one of his subordinates, "so everything was justified." He tells the court that Frans spread the word around the motor vehicle facility that a clandestine organization was being set up to punish political offenders. Frans hinted that the highest echelons of the military stood behind this initiative, but never named names. Although no one was privy to the ins and outs of the organization, everyone wanted to join it. "It was precisely that secrecy that attracted us," says a sergeant. "That mysterious hit squad was on everyone's lips."

Then Johan Peterse's lawyer takes over. Peterse is the man

who delivered the bomb to the Prinsengracht and subsequently tossed the remaining two bombs into the canal. He, too, accuses Frans of being the instigator. I reluctantly retype his statement: "My client is a man bound by loyalty, as this country expects of its sons. A solid, balanced man and an exemplary soldier. My client was decorated in 1945 for his wartime bravery. This bombing tragedy was a fateful accident. My client believed that all four potential targets were traitors who, through this secret mission, would receive the punishment they had thus far evaded."

Once I've retyped that second sheet, I file it away, irritated. This is not what I was hoping for. I want to read how Frans testified in his own words that the mission went differently than planned, that he was shocked to hear there were innocent victims, that he'd been searching for the right words ever since to express his regret to the survivors.

I turn to the next page and sigh as I wrestle through yet more statements painting Frans as a vindictive authoritarian. Just as I am starting to suspect that the court stenographer had ignored his words or that there's a page missing, I reach this passage: "Captain van Heemstra remained silent during the hearing. He always maintained his innocence, even after all the evidence had been presented. When, during his arrest, he was asked how he felt about the death of that girl, who in no way whatsoever was involved in the affair, he replied: 'These things happen.'"

My stomach contracts when I read those last words. I skim the rest of the page in search of any other statements from Frans. An answer, an explanation, a retort. But not a word. I'm going to have to make do with "These things happen."

Collateral damage. I hope none of the victims' family were in the courtroom. And if they were, I hope there was no eye contact when those words were read aloud. I look around the white table, wonder how often the others feel disgust when they read their dossiers, and how they all appear to maintain their self-control amid so many upsetting revelations.

Limbs push against the inside of my belly. The baby's stretching. I place my hands on the lump that might be his head but could just as well be his backside. There's no getting around it. Frans was unscrupulous. Guilty. An outlaw.

I wearily take the last crumpled page from the table, and within a few sentences I stumble onto yet another perspective on the events.

Two and a half hours before the court reached its verdict, a certain Major Baak holds "an emotional speech" that is taken down as witness testimony. "Major Baak," writes the stenographer, "describes, with great empathy and drama, in both bearing and voice, the qualities of these men and the tragedy of their lives.

"This is a matter" (says the major) "on the edge of resistance and on the line separating the old days from the new. Where does resistance begin, and where does it end? Does it end at the moment of liberation? Shouldn't there be a distinction between *actual* and *psychological* resistance? For these men, the Resistance was far from over, and seeing as they *were* the Resistance all those years, we could say that if they felt it was not over, then for them it indeed *wasn't* over. And if it was not over, how deserving of punishment is an act that a year earlier would have earned them a commendation?

"Can war turn into peace from one day to the next?

"Can a man turn from a hero into a murderer in a single night?"

Directly underneath are the results of the psychiatric examination Frans underwent while in custody. The diagnosis: "Resistance psychosis." What the symptoms or indications of such a condition are, no one says.

And then there is one last witness. According to a sergeant from Frans's barracks, the captain had been in contact with several men from the Dutch security services who had similar views on bringing unindicted war criminals to justice. They complained at the impossibility of prosecuting "these folks" due to lack of direct evidence of treason. They discussed setting up a national network of vigilantes and fantasized about "large-scale military action." Ex-Resistance men versus the traitors. The sergeant claims to have heard from a reliable source that the security services themselves supported the attack. "Captain van Heemstra will decline to tell you anything about it himself," he says. "It was a strictly confidential mission."

This fresh take on Frans's silence renews my hopes of heroism. Loyal to his mission until the very end. This is how I have always pictured Bommenneef: steadfast of character, dedicated to the fight for justice, ready to take the fall rather than betray his comrades.

But the judge is not swayed by the possible involvement of the security services, nor by Major Baak's plea.

Frans is deemed a "danger to the state, and unfit for continued military status—unfit to the degree that he must be permanently prohibited from serving in the armed forces." He is sentenced to thirteen years' imprisonment, minus time already served. Ate De Boer gets eleven and a half years, Johan Peterse seven.

As far as the judge is concerned, the war is over, and thus the Resistance as well.

I gather up the yellowed sheets of paper. Even though I have retyped them all, it feels wrong to put them back in the box and abandon them to the indifference of that cavernous depot.

Would anyone notice if I just slid them into my bag? I pick up the stack, glance cautiously around the table, and see that the security man has his eye on me.

I briefly consider ignoring him, jamming the papers into my bag and walking off. What does it matter? What's the point of wasting storage room for another seventy years with a dossier that interests no one except me?

But the security guard casts me a cautionary glance. I look at my tablemates, silently bent over their stories. Suddenly the white table has become a prison, the security man the warden, and history our punishment.

I place the papers back in the box, turn it in to the Afghan hound, and walk toward the security gates at the exit. I turn to wave goodbye to Herman, but he gestures that I should wait for him. I shake my head. Fatigue is streaming through my body. I do not want to wait. I want to find evidence that supports that last testimony, confirmation that the assignment came from some higher-up, and that Frans kept quiet out of allegiance, not callousness.

I ask at the counter if there is a dossier on the National Security Services in the 1940s. I have to start somewhere.

"What year?"

"1946."

She types something in, clicks a few times with her mouse. "No dossier, but there's a book."

She gets up and walks over to the low bookcase across from her counter. Her finger skims along the rows of books, and she pulls a gigantic square tome off the shelf. *History of the Dutch Domestic Security Services.* "You can't take it with you," she says, "but I can hold it for you at the counter for as long as you need it."

12 WEEKS LEFT

EVERY MORNING AFTER D closes the door behind
him, I shuffle off to the station, board the train to The Hague,
and then pant my way the last hundred meters to the National
Archive. I'm now one of the regulars. Every morning the same
empty chair is waiting for me at the big white table. The days
follow a regular pattern. I collect the book at the counter, smile
to the Afghan hound as I walk to the reading room, nod briefly
at the twins and then to the security guard, who points with
raised eyebrows at his Post-its, to which I respond by shaking
my head and showing him the book: no "extraordinary jurisdiction." I read, and if I'm too tired, which is often the case, I
take pictures of the pages with my phone so I can read them

later at home. At 11:30 sharp Herman slides his chair back and we take a break, usually still going through our reading material, at the coffee bar. I leave at three o'clock so that I'm in bed when D gets home. To make it look plausible I put a mug with an inch of tepid tea and a plate with crumbs next to the bed.

I wrestle my way through the first half of the book in three days. I read about the formation of the Dutch intelligence service in 1919, after Pieter Jelles Troelstra, the dreaded socialist leader who had called for a revolution following World War I, had managed to rustle up three thousand communists for a demonstration. I read about the "red scare" and the "German threat." I get distracted, doze off. The pages are too big and the type too small; I wander past dates and facts that have nothing to do with my story, but I don't dare skip anything for fear I might miss that one paragraph about the secret plot.

Only on day 4 do I encounter names I recognize from the dossier. Military men who testified at the trial, the ones mentioned as being involved in the potential conspiracy. I read about the tangle of clubs and organizations who claimed to belong to the postwar secret service. The "Resistance Council," the vigilante units, the intelligence wing of the "Stoottroepen," the "Dutch Secret Service." Various groups of men who felt that their role in the Resistance gave them the right to determine the direction of the postwar Netherlands. I meander through pages and pages of wiretapping, conflicts, offshoots, and subgroups—who knew what a messy business peace could be? And then, halfway through the book, there it is in black-and-white: the name "Frans van Heemstra." I take my cell phone, photograph the entire chapter to be able to refer back to it at home, and start reading.

It describes a "Special Missions Committee" with which

Frans was in contact in the period preceding the bombing. "A secret organization for combatting communism." Their plan was ambitious: to consolidate all the vigilante units as a show of strength against the "leftists." If this is true, then the aim of settling the score with Dutch traitors was no more than a ploy to rouse the vigilantes and revive ex-Resistance heroes' combativeness. But nowhere do I find any proof for this theory. What I do find are descriptions of extravagant but never-executed plans, rumors, failed shadow armies. And then the paragraph that takes me so by surprise that I have to reread it three times before the reality of it sinks in.

Frans was said to have been part of the founding, in late 1945, of a "neue Abwehr," a right-wing terrorist organization bent on joining forces with ex-Nazis to combat the left-wing danger. One of their plans, I read, was to spring him from prison so that he could go to Germany and work for a Nazi spy.

I turn the page, hoping that this paragraph will be subsequently disproved. But no. Frans was actually planning to team up with a man who, two years earlier, he would have fought to the death. So much for an inner moral law.

Across from me, Herman slides back his chair. Coffee break. I close my book, follow him slowly to the foyer. Just hope he doesn't ask anything. I have no desire to share my astonishment about Nazi spies and the "new defense" with Herman. It's one thing to privately own up to one's own misjudgment, but to share it is quite another. I would have to come up with another story, and I don't know yet what that is, or should be. When we reach the coffee bar, I want to say I'm going to skip our break today, that I'm going straight home. But before I can get a word out, Herman smacks a stack of papers on the table.

"Eureka!"

"What?"

"I've found it. The connection, the line, the thread."

I gingerly pick up the top sheet.

A list of names, Frans van Heemstra nearly at the bottom, and above him, Herman Witte.

"That's me," Herman says enthusiastically, "or I should say, that's my father."

I skim the rest of the names, try to figure out what it is I'm looking at. Again Herman beats me to the punch. "It's a list of men who were held on remand in December 1946."

"So . . . ?" I give Herman a questioning look, not yet certain how to phrase what I want to say.

"They were in the same cell block!"

Herman takes a minicarton of chocolate milk out of his breast pocket and stabs the straw triumphantly through the little foil dot. I look at him and back to the list. So my uneasiness when he asked about François recently was not unfounded. He has sucked Bommenneef into his father's story, or vice versa. Whichever it is, he has appropriated Cousin Bomber. He will read the dossiers, will know everything I know and probably more, because he's just better at looking for and finding things in this labyrinth than I am. I'll no longer be able to decide what to share with him and what not to, I can no longer lie, no longer put things off till later. Now there is a witness: in every detective show on TV, that marks the beginning of the end.

I put the sheet back on the table. I can't come up with anything better than: "I don't want this."

Herman looks at me, perplexed. "Do you know what this means? Our stories have coalesced."

"Yes," I say. "I know that, and I don't want it."

"But now I can help you," he protests. He suddenly appears helpless, with his chocolate milk and his stupid stack of papers. My eyes cloud over, for a split second everything goes dark, and then a burning rage shoots from my toes up to the crown of my head. I want to hurl Herman's papers through the room but catch myself just in time. So this is what they mean about hormonal mood swings. Breathe deeply. Count to ten. It doesn't help. All the worries and frustrations of the past weeks are clenched in my chest. I don't want yet more empty spaces and question marks on the map, or the chaos of Herman's web that has no beginning and no end, or the craziness in my own head, or this indeterminate body that only grows and grows.

I snap at Herman that he mustn't go grabbling around in my research as a distraction from his own fruitless quest, that the box of stuff about his father is just an excuse to stick his nose into a past he has nothing to do with. "I don't have the time for this nonsense," I say. Off to the left I see the barista take cover behind the bar.

I look at Herman's two big, scared eyes.

"What are you just standing there for?"

My voice echoes through the foyer. The barista ducks down behind the counter, pretending to inspect the refrigerators. His head just sticks out above the countertop, as though he is in a battlefield trench. I turn back to Herman and poke a trembling finger into his chest. "You know what your problem is? You're afraid you take after your father. You lure all these stories into your web, try to make everyone an accessory to your father's crime, because you're afraid of your genes, afraid that his betrayal and contempt for other people's lives might have rubbed off on you. You're scared to death that because you've got his blood you might make the same choices he did, that deep down, you're a bad person."

For a brief moment I see myself from a bird's-eye perspective: a pregnant woman with swollen legs, standing in a gigantic foyer kicking up a ruckus about nothing—no, not about nothing, about keeping her story intact, about keeping Bommenneef alive, about not turning her hero over to some old pensioner who, with his little juice cartons and infantile smile, is trying to appropriate her family history.

I see my own stupefaction reflected in Herman's face. I stop ranting, I see how he searches in vain for words, gathers up the papers, as though he'll find something there in that long list of men whose glances might have crossed once on their way to or from their cell. Men who had nothing to do with one another except that history happened to plop them down in the same place at the same time, just like us now in this great big empty foyer.

Herman totters slightly, shifts from one foot to the other. I want to grab him by the shoulders, sit him down, and order him a coffee; I want him to go away and quit meddling with Bommenneef; I don't know what I want. Behind me I hear the barista rummage in a cabinet. He puts on a CD to break this awful silence. The Buena Vista Social Club, that'll do. I turn and march off. I try to put some anger into my gait, so that Herman doesn't see how embarrassed I am. "Sorry," I mumble as I head for the revolving door. "Sorry, sorry, sorry"—I keep mumbling it until I reach the station, until I'm on the train, until we start moving, "sorry, sorry," so quietly that no one hears.

11 WEEKS LEFT

A WEEK HAS GONE by in silence. I lie on my bed and watch the treetops slowly turn red. My blood pressure has risen steadily since my last visit to the archive. I take pills and rest, I read and electrocute the mosquitoes that rose from the dead the day after the exterminator had eradicated them. I keep swelling up, faster now. The elastic in my socks digs into my ankles, my ring only fits my pinky now.

We drive to the hospital every other day. By now I know the routine of the blood pressure meter by heart: the crescendo of the hum, the rhythm of the beeps, first slower, then speeding up, until the final score appears on the little screen, followed by the nurse's shaking head: still too high.

D leaves me behind every morning with orders not to move until he's back from work. I ask him if his concern is for me or for the baby.

"I don't think there's a difference anymore," he says.

Today he comes home early. "We have to celebrate reaching the magical milestone of the third trimester," he'd said before leaving.

"That was last week," I replied.

"All the more reason to celebrate," he said with a laugh.

The chance that the baby will be born without too many defects grows by the day. As does the baby himself: the length of an eggplant, the weight of a thick wool sweater, say the websites. He can blink, cough, and dream (although what in God's name a fetus has to dream about, nobody says). I click further to the next few weeks. Ear of corn, turnip, cauliflower, pumpkin. They warn for patches of pigment brought on by the hormones; the official term is "pregnancy mask"—what a terrific concept, being able to hide behind your pregnancy. The website's weekly overview includes comments from mothers-to-be who complain of swelling, welts, cramps, and the baby's kicking. "It's domestic violence, pure and simple," one woman writes. Another tells how the somersaults going on in her belly gave her two bruised ribs. Underneath, the mother of a two-year-old wrote, "It doesn't end there. This morning my kid gave me a bloody nose. He wasn't even angry, he was just flailing about."

I think of Herman a lot. I'd like to phone him and apologize, but I don't have his number. I imagine him sitting in the reading room, still nonplussed by my outburst. Who knows, maybe he and the barista gossip about me. What would they say? Hysterical. Hormonal.

I lie in bed studying the pages I photographed from *History of the Dutch Domestic Security Services*. Nothing in the book indicates that the secret plans Bommenneef whispered about were anything more than the megalomaniac fantasies of men frustrated with their role in postwar Netherlands.

What does crop up is the diagnosis mentioned in Frans's psychiatric report: "Resistance psychosis."

There's no official definition of the term anywhere, but it does appear in a book by Simon Vestdijk, *Liberation Festival*, written in 1949, which I found online. In it, one character, a Resistance hero, explains the basis for his psychosis: "the fear, and everything that went with it, at least meant we weren't bored. We had a goal. Even those who were just afraid and otherwise didn't do a blessed thing had a goal."

I read the novel in a single afternoon. After the war, the hero in the book is terrified that he'll die of boredom, so he plans two attacks, both of which fail. In the end he has no choice but to return, disillusioned, to everyday life.

Liberation Festival could have been Bommenneef's story, except that with him, one of the attacks did succeed. It's as though Frans, just like Vestdijk's hero, was determined to keep the war going, cost what it may. Or, better put, to be forever ending it. But to accomplish that, the war had to carry on. Frans wouldn't, or couldn't, reconcile himself with a tedious peace.

I return to the online newspaper archive where I had earlier tracked down reports of the bombing and try to picture the peace in which Frans found himself. Alongside the articles about the bomb are items about the poor quality of hand soap, advertisements for nylon stockings, the announcement of the opening of a new theater in the north of the country, an ad for a brand-new board game called Reconstruction, the news that Dutch cyclists unanimously opted for a bike with extra-sturdy tires, and that the nostalgic ballad "Bloesem van Seringen" was the hit of 1947. There are some items I have to read twice before I understand what they're getting at, because I recognize the words but not the context. "Nieuw Schoonbeek oil line opened." "Northern round-trips begun." "Flezkis to the East Indies." And then there are the news items I had expected to be there but aren't. Nothing about the Holocaust, nothing about concentration camp survivors, nothing about the extermination of the Jews, about confiscated property, or about the exhausted Dutch survivors of the Japanese internment camps. Nothing about the facts I learned to associate with those years. Hand soap. Nylon stockings. Theaters. A bombing.

For Frans, the wound had to stay fresh. He longed for the days when death nipped at his heels, when every cigarette or woman could be your last. Resistance psychosis.

I email three psychiatrist acquaintances about this syndrome. Not one of them has heard of it. They do agree that extreme stress factors can unhinge a person to the extent that it could trigger an existing susceptibility to psychosis, with the possibility of a genuine psychosis as a result. They also agree that there could be hundreds of other explanations for Frans's behavior.

One of them suggests I study the profiles of the young terrorists who currently dominate our news headlines, and points to certain possible similarities: enmity against society, the feeling of not being taken seriously, and the lack of existential meaning, all of which can make one receptive to radical ideology.

I'm startled by that word: "terrorist." I have never stopped to consider how that attack would be seen today. A bomb, three fatalities. Is it possible that our little family legend is equivalent to what nowadays makes us afraid to fly or congregate in crowded spaces? That the victims always get forgotten, even though the bombing was once front-page news? Is it possible that seventy years from now, a niece of one of today's terrorists will get a standing ovation for her show-and-tell performance about her heroic uncle? Am I that niece?

I know there are a hundred other stories to choose from for my son. The one about his great-great-aunt who flew to Rhodesia in a tiny airplane in 1939 to help convert African women but ended up falling head over heels for a tribal chief and living with him in a hut for five years. Or the one about another distant uncle who died in his mistress's bed and was smuggled out of the house by his two sons, and that they drove around for hours looking for a dignified place to leave his body. Or the story of my great-grandfather, who was executed by firing squad in Zutphen two months before liberation, and for whom there is a small white brick cross at a parking area along the IJssel River.

"If you want a hero, why not look into that story?" asked an uncle who wasn't so keen on my obsession with twice-removed Bommenneef. I did not know how to reply, but now I do: because it's too close. I know too many details of that story. And because of his closeness, my great-grandfather is too much person, not enough hero.

So many stories—but I wanted *this* one. Because of the ring, because of his last wish. But it was also a matter of proportion, of being just the right distance.

I follow the flock of starlings that dips and dives in a synchronized show in the evening light above our square. What was it that Herman said about those old school prints? The artist thought he was drawing history, but in the end, he was only drawing himself.

For the first time, I think of Bommenneef's mother. Of the months she carried him in her belly in the summer of 1909. What did she expect of her son? That he would be better and smarter than she. That he would achieve the things she had left undone. That he would become a necessary new presence among everything that was already there, the crown on the creation, or at least a warm, cuddly body to embrace and, later, to lean on. A mother expects all sorts of things, but not that her child becomes a mass murderer.

"Knock knock, who's there? It's Adolf's heartchen knocking," wrote Wisława Szymborska in "Hitler's First Photograph." Little Adolf is a precious angel and mommy's sunshine, a little fellow in his itty-bitty robe. Can you ever entertain the notion that with the birth of your child you multiply not life, but death? Perhaps that's the only way to give the baby a fair chance. The only way not to saddle him with expectations he cannot achieve, to give him the right to exist, regardless of what that existence is. He might hurt, destroy, fail, maybe even murder. At the very least, you have to accept that as a possibility. Allowing death as well as life.

10 WEEKS LEFT

I BOLT AWAKE WITH an intense cramp in my left calf, a whiplash, a snakebite. In a panic I jiggle my leg back and forth, try to shake out the pain, but it only makes it worse. I knead and push with both hands. The muscles feel as hard as steel cables. The leg starts quivering as though possessed.

I jab D with my elbow. "Wake up," I pant. "My leg. My leg!"

Slowly, D sits up, searches for my leg in the dark, clamps his big warm hand around my calf.

"Here?"

"Yes!"

He calmly massages the muscles. The quivering subsides, the pain recedes.

"Okay now?"

"Thanks." But he doesn't even hear me. I don't know any-one who falls asleep as easily as D does. He closes his eyes and within seconds, he's gone. Total abandon. I look at my phone. Four o'clock. I google "cramp + calf + pregnancy."

It turns out to be yet another standard malaise. Abnormal circulation, mineral deficiency, too much or too little exercise. I can't get back to sleep, which 24baby.nl says can be because of a hormonal disturbance, and according to mammanet.nl (which I still inevitably read as "mammoth net") is due to the stress of a child being on the way. Maybe it's just the mosquitoes. I swipe the electric racket around a bit, see the occasional flash, and at four thirty I decide to go downstairs and wait for the day to begin. It's dead quiet outside, that strange in-between time when night becomes day. Above the rooftops it's already getting light. Everything looks lonely this morning: the neighbors' overloaded balconies, the empty birdhouses in the backyards, the motionless underwear on our washing rack. Even the baby hasn't budged for hours. I am alone with things, in a world that is not ready to awaken.

The mail flap clatters. I walk downstairs, pick up the news-paper, and skim the front page. Terror alert. Influx of refugees. In the middle section, an obituary for a Resistance woman who died yesterday, a hundred years old. World War II seems to be getting a lot of attention these days. Maybe it's my selective perspective, but I see that war everywhere, just like I now also see pregnant women all over the place.

Accompanying the article is a large picture of the Resistance woman, crooked as a corkscrew. She's seated, wearing a bright-pink sweater, her hands packed in dark-blue wool mittens.

According to the article, she was one of the few females in the Resistance and was part of a gang that after the war murdered an engineer from Leiden, assuming he had been a collaborator. He turned out to be innocent. The engineer, writes the obituary's author, was one of the many victims of "similar misjudgments." I wonder if Frans's bomb victims are on this journalist's list. Three of the many. It sounds so innocent: a bad call.

The murder tormented the woman all her life. She admitted to it at the age of ninety-six. The obituary recalls an interview that questions the reasoning behind the belated admission. Did she just want to clear her conscience? Or with death looming, was there fear of a last judgment, a gate, a God?

"Being close to death," the woman replied, "puts you at your most honest, perhaps your only really honest moment. You've got nothing left to lose."

Suddenly I know which moment in Frans's life I would choose if I had Billy Pilgrim's gift of time travel: his last day. The hours before his death in that beastly hot Spanish seaside resort, where he expired, sick and alone. I would drive him to the harbor, order calamari at a small outdoor café, and wait for him to talk. It's exactly what this story needs. After all that's been made up and kept back: an honest moment. An open space to which all the routes, side roads, and detours lead.

I look at my phone. Quarter after eight. Late enough to call, I reckon. I tap in B's number. If anyone knows about Bommenneef's last hours, it will be her.

After the fifth ring she answers with a sleepy voice, and sighs when she hears my name.

"Do you know what time it is?"

"Sorry. Should I call back later?"

"Never mind. Haven't you finished your scavenger hunt yet?"

"I haven't found what I'm after."

I ask her about Frans's end. "What were his last words? Was there a letter?"

"If you really want to know," she says, irked, "it was dreadful. The marine corps man who cared for him said he was impossible. The last few months he was a disheveled mess. At night he was a ghost on wheels. He cursed, he scratched the legs he no longer had. He died while the marine was back here for a few days. The man from the corner grocery kept an eye on things and brought supplies. Juan Carlos. He sat next to him when he died."

"Did this Juan Carlos ever say anything about it?"

"No."

"Nothing?"

"Just that he died. In his wheelchair."

"But nothing about last words? A message? A declaration of some kind?"

"Not that I know of."

"Nothing about the ring he sent to Holland?"

"No idea."

I picture Frans in his wheelchair, sleepless and swearing. It must have been his conscience keeping him awake. A ghost from the past that goaded him through the house. But even if B knows anything, she's not going to talk.

The road to Frans's final, honest moment is a dead end. For a moment I consider going to Spain, looking up Juan Carlos, asking him how it went. But I stop myself. Out of the question. What if the Spanish sun pushes up my blood pressure further than it already is, that my water breaks there in Vinaròs, that our son is born on the very spot where Bommenneef died. Besides, D wouldn't let me go. I look up Vinaròs on my iPhone. It's not far from Barcelona. I also check the airlines' rules about flying when pregnant. Depending on the airline, it's either thirty-two or thirty-six weeks. I look up fares. Just to see if it would even be possible, I tell myself. As the vacation website calculates the fare, another cramp shoots through my calf. I try to repeat what D did—massage, stay calm—but my hands aren't as warm or as big as his, and the pain bites into my muscles. All I can do is wait. Slowly, ever so slowly, the cramp recedes. The tickets are affordable. The vacation site gives the weather in Vinaròs an 8.8 out of 10. I move the cursor to the icon in the middle of the screen: "Book Now." Even if I did dare, D would flip out at the very idea. And not only him: my sisters, my parents, my friends would unanimously forbid it.

I scroll through the photos of the *History of the Dutch Domestic Security Services*. Reopen the emails from the psychiatrists and again get mired on the word "terrorist." I have to find a new route, one that runs straight through the white area on the map, otherwise I won't make it on time.

The doorbell rings. Startled, I look up from my phone. Eight thirty. At the door are two men, one tall and one short, wearing thick rubber boots and carrying something that resembles a giant pump.

"Pest control!" the tall one cries. D appears at the top of the stairs, his head still clouded in sleep. "Shit . . . forgot. I'd asked new exterminators to come." While D gets dressed and I make coffee, the men inspect every corner of the house and conclude that there are indeed a lot of mosquitoes. I tell him about the last, failed, attempt to get rid of them.

"You've got to tackle the source, not the bugs," the tall one says. He wants to inspect the crawl space. "Where there are mosquitoes, there's water," he continues, "and vice versa." The short one nods earnestly at everything his tall colleague says, as though he is proclaiming great philosophical truths.

I yell up to D: "Do we have a crawl space?"

"Of course," he shouts back.

"Look under the doormat," says the one.

"I'll do it," says the other, eyeing my belly.

He pulls the mat aside, revealing, to my surprise, a hatch I've never seen in the two years we've lived here.

I bend over and pull on the metal ring. There's not much to see down there—a dark, low cavern under the floor—but still, it's weird that I've lived here for two years without any idea it even existed. "Does this run under the entire house?"

Instead of answering, the men sink to their knees and—as though they're following some predetermined choreography—simultaneously stick their head in the opening. "There's water," the small one says. "Lots of water," adds the tall one. "And lots of mosquitoes," says the small one in turn. Bert and Ernie. I look at the two headless bent-over bodies. If you were to dig a tunnel straight through the earth from our kitchen, a friend told us at the housewarming party, you'd come out in the South Pacific. It made me dizzy, that deep-blue antipode of our house. Water, sun, and sharks opposite our tidy, quiet life. But first there's the crawl space, a buffer zone filled with bugs and damp.

The men hang a rubber hose into the opening and hook up the pump. The short one pushes a button.

"And now?" I ask.

"We wait," says the tall one.

I go upstairs to my desk, open Google Maps on my laptop, and zoom in on Vinaròs. The street view images show a surprisingly empty cityscape. I drag my little virtual yellow man to the seaside boulevard: Avinguda de Francisco José Balada. The beach, too, looks forsaken. A bright-blue sky, light-gray waves. Right up near the boulevard, a family (Germans, I automatically assume) sits in a large hollow eating sandwiches; otherwise the place is deserted. If I scroll the viewer to the left, I see a group of people, their pant legs rolled up, walking along the high-water mark. On their side, the sky is overcast—the photos were clearly not taken on the same day, and maybe these people weren't ever really on the beach at all, but photoshopped into the picture by Google to make the beach scene complete. I click away from the coast, wander past light-pink villas and low-rise white vacation apartment complexes. Twice, I pass a corner grocery, and in one of them I notice the silhouette of a man behind the window.

"We're done!" A loud voice from downstairs startles me out of my Spanish ramble. "All taken care of!"

They leave the hatch open when they leave. D sends me back to bed, but as soon as he's left for work, I'm back at my laptop.

I spend the morning rereading the notes I've taken since the beginning of my search. I wander, word by word, toward the dead end where I've now arrived. And gradually a new strategy unfolds.

Until now I have invariably approached the case from the same perspective: that of the culprits, and the route that led them to Prinsengracht 266. How about if I open the door? Inspect what was behind it? The staircase, the lost lives? I open the document with the list of injuries and Maria Johanna's statement. There must be family members, children, and grandchildren of the victims who have some knowledge of the incident. The other side of the story has surely been passed in the same game of telephone through their families. They'll remember what my family has forgotten. Maybe a distant niece on their side has also delved into the bombing. We only have to meet to fill in the blanks and reach the correct conclusions. I need a family tree, names, addresses. I need the help of someone who is better and quicker at this than I am.

9 WEEKS LEFT

I SEE HERMAN SITTING in the coffee nook as I pass through the revolving door. Before I can call out to him, he glances up—a calm, dry look—and waves both hands above his head—*I'm not waving, I'm drowning*—what song is that from again?

As I waddle toward him, he goes over to the counter and orders a coffee and a doppio. The barista, having spotted me, puts on the Buena Vista Social Club, just to be on the safe side. "You've changed," Herman says when I sit down next to him.

"Fatter," I say.

"A tiny bit."

"A huge tiny bit. Three and a half pounds in four days. My body sucks up every drop of fluid that crosses its path."

Herman laughs, and I laugh along, relieved that our reunion is going so smoothly.

"Are you okay?" he asks. Now he sounds worried.

I nod. I don't feel like bringing up my blood pressure; I have to make good use of the little time I've got left. In three hours D will come home and my mother will show up with a pot of chicken soup. If I'm not back in bed by then, they're likely to put me under house arrest until the delivery.

My entire body tells me what a bad idea this was; even that short walk from the station has worn me out. But I didn't know how else to reach Herman, and without him I'll never round this off on time.

"I need you," I say.

Herman nods, as though he expected it.

"And I apologize for . . . ," I add. "I'm . . ."

"Never mind."

The barista cautiously—I'll bet he's afraid of riling me—sets our coffees on the counter.

Herman leaps up, returns with the cups. For a few seconds we sit in silence. Then he starts to talk. His voice is quiet and melancholy.

"After you walked off last time, I drove down to Margraten, to the Netherlands American Cemetery and Memorial. To the grave I adopted: Johnny, an American kid who's been lying there in the Limburg hills for seventy years. He was seventeen. *Seventeen*. And standing there among all those white crosses, I . . ." His voice trails off, and he looks at me with watery eyes.

I'm afraid he's going to cry, and that I'll start crying, too, because I cry over everything these days. But Herman does not cry. He looks in silence at his coffee. I want to touch him, comfort him, but I don't dare.

"Maybe you should adopt something else," I say. "A tree. Or an Oxfam goat. A foster child, if need be. Adopting a grave is so . . . so . . ."

"Sad?"

"So desolate. Adoption's supposed to be about hope, about the future. Investing in a new life."

"In a pan-dimensional world, Johnny could have been my son. I stood there among all those headstones and thought: this war will never, never, never be over."

I reach out my hand, unsure of where to place it. On his shoulder? His cheek? It lands on his elbow, where it awkwardly remains.

"It's been seventy years," I say. "Pretty soon that war will be ancient history."

Herman glumly stirs his coffee. "You have no idea. Officially I didn't experience it firsthand, but the war was still going when I was born, it was in my mother's milk, it was in my diapers. It's got nothing to do with exact dates or with how much time has passed."

"I'm sorry," I say.

He chuckles. "That doesn't make any sense."

"I know. It's the best I could come up with."

Herman bends over and picks up the worn attaché case from the floor under his chair. "Here, I've got something for you." He places a sheet of paper, a photocopy, on the table. It's got two columns, on the left a list of the names of the Boer family: François, Greetje, their son, and a daughter I haven't yet come across in the archive. The right-hand column gives their date and place of birth.

"Exactly what I was looking for," I say, surprised.

"I thought so," Herman replies. "Boer's children might still be alive, otherwise you could use their data to trace the grandchildren. It's taking a bit longer to find Jacoba's family tree without her birthdate."

Herman gives me a guilty look and laughs in that irresistible adolescent giggle of his.

"If you think it's too much, just say so, but I've got one more thing for you."

He digs under the little cartons of orange juice and pulls out a small stack of crinkled papers. On the top is a photo of Prinsengracht 266, just after the bombing. It's smaller than I remember when my grandmother showed it to me. On the ground floor is a narrow garage. "Prinsengracht Autos Motorcycles Bicycles" is painted in block letters on the brickwork. Two men in trilby hats crouch on the sidewalk, inspecting a large pile of glass. Next to them are two other men, one of them a uniformed policeman. The door to number 266 is open, offering a glimpse of the entrance hall, with its white tiles with a thin black border. It's what the two passersby saw when, the previous evening, they put their deadly package on the stairs. A half-charred curtain flaps from an upstairs window.

"From The Hague photo bank," Herman says. "They tore down the house in 2002, by the way." I take the next paper from under the photo: a ground plan of the street. Herman points to a small orange peaked-roof icon.

"Now it's a shopping center with underground parking."

I look at the little orange roof. Do you suppose that there's anything left under the concrete? A splinter that didn't get swept up, and then got washed into the ground by the rainwater? Tiny bits of François's or Jacoba's DNA? How much of you stays behind in the place where you die?

I touch the photograph, the shattered glass. "Did you know that Boer wasn't such a criminal after all? There were rumors, but nothing was proven."

Herman nods. "Fish and birds. I've read the dossier. But that bird-catching isn't as innocent as it sounds. Carrier pigeons were the forgotten heroes of World War II. They flew through barrages and conflagrations with information strapped to their feet, they were on board airplanes and submarines. They were spies, soldiers, freedom fighters. Did you know that after the war, thirty pigeons were given a commendation? That's why the Germans sent people out to catch and kill them. People with bird-catching skills, like François. So no, nothing was proven, and maybe nothing did happen, but maybe it did. The question is, which pigeon got caught in his net?"

This new information throws me off. Just as I was getting used to the idea of an innocent François sacrificed on the altar of belligerence, this crops up.

"My god," I sigh, "what is it going to take to reach the right conclusion?"

"Everything."

My telephone vibrates in my bag. It'll be D, or one of my sisters or parents; someone is worried because I haven't returned their call quickly enough and will worry even more when I do answer and am clearly not in bed. I check the screen: seven missed calls. Three from D, three from my mother, one from my sister. I scribble my contact information on the Prinsen-gracht street plan and tuck it back into Herman's bag.

"I have to go."

Herman nods. "How much longer now?"

"Nine weeks."

"I'll make sure you get what you're looking for."

Back home, I take out the blood pressure meter my father gave me, strap the sleeve around my upper arm, push the button. The machine's hum makes me think of the mosquitoes. With the water pumped out of the crawl space, the mosquitoes gradually disappeared, and for some strange reason I miss them, because it's suddenly so quiet in the bedroom and without the distraction of the buzzing I'm free to agonize to my heart's content. In twenty-three short beeps the meter counts down to today's reading. I'm surprised by how low it is: lower than yesterday, lower than even this morning. So the search is not the cause of my stress; in fact, it's a kind of medicine. I lie down on the bed, call D, my mother, and my sister, and reassure them all.

HERMAN IS A man of his word. That same evening he emails me a batch of new information. After the bombing, he writes, François's son emigrated to a village outside Cape Town and started a family. He attaches an Excel document he found online: a list of the estates of deceased South African farmers. About halfway down is the name François Guillaume Jacques Boer, who died in 2007. "I'm guessing this was Boer's grandson," Herman writes. "He had children, but I can't locate them right now." Boer's seventeen-year-old daughter stayed in the Netherlands and married a man from Zaandam. She, too, says Herman, is deceased.

On Facebook I locate a South African student named François

Boer. From his profile picture I'd say he's about twenty, so it would have to be the great-grandson, or even the great-great-grandson. I send a friend request—he accepts it immediately—and a few minutes later François the 3rd, or 4th, or 5th, initiates a chat with me.

François: Hi!

I'm startled by the small window at the bottom of my screen. That name, the bouncing ellipsis that indicates he is typing. What am I supposed to write to François Boer's namesake? Does he know who I am? Is he aware of the story?

François: Are we related? My family is from the Netherlands.

Me: I know.

For a moment nothing happens, no ellipsis. He's waiting for more but I don't know how to begin.

François: Mysterious . . .

Help. Pretty soon he'll think I'm flirting with him.

Me: Are you the great-grandson of François Boer, son of François Boer from Holland?

François: Add one more François, and that's me!

Me: I'm writing you because . . .

My hand pauses above the keyboard. I should have thought this through first.

François is getting impatient.

François: ?? . . .

Okay, don't chicken out now. Kick in the door, march up the stairs, grab history by the hair, and look it straight in the eye. I don't know what you call your grandfather's cousin in English, so to make it easy I call him an uncle: "Because my uncle was responsible for the bomb attack that killed your great-great-grandparents."

Too direct? Maybe. But how does one casually bring up a generations-old murder in a Facebook chat?

For a while it's quiet in the southern hemisphere.

Then he answers with four question marks.

I ask François the 3rd or 4th or whatever if he knows anything about the wartime history of the Boer family. The ellipsis dances, he types, erases his message, and starts again. It pops up five minutes later. I don't know much, he writes, except that my great-grandfather's brother was in the Resistance. In 1943 he killed a Nazi and went into hiding after that.

And your great-great-grandfather?

No idea, he replies. I don't know anything about an attack. Was he a Resistance hero too? After this last question are three smileys with hopeful expressions.

I don't think so, I respond.

Frowning smiley.

"Do you know what happened on the evening of December 5, 1946?"

"No," he answers. All he knows is that as a baby, his grandfather's hearing was damaged during a German bombardment. The house was on fire, he writes, and his great-grandmother jumped out the window with his grandfather in her arms.

A German bombardment. The Boer family's telephone game has turned Bommenneef's attack into an enemy blitz. No pigeon nets, no liquidation, no dossier in the Extraordinary Jurisdiction archive, but the victims of world history.

I thank François and close the chat.

The descendants of Boer's daughter are easier to trace. She had a son and a daughter; both are still alive and live in the vicinity of The Hague. The son is on Facebook and accepts my friend request. I send a message, more circumspect this time. He's a generation closer to the murder, which I imagine makes a difference. I tell him about my research, say I'm looking for the other side of the story. An hour later, he has read it. He does not respond.

Another email from Herman comes in: a link to the long, narrow family tree of an American professor, taken from a genealogy website. The tree is rooted in eighteenth-century Zeeland. On a branch of a branch is the small and lonely mention of Jacoba, followed by her dates.

I try to formulate my email to the professor as cautiously as possible.

Dear Mr. Van der Wal, I have recently been researching a bomb attack in 1946 that killed Jacoba Visser, a distant aunt of yours. A family member of mine was involved and I'm trying to find out more about the attack and its aftermath.

Again, no reply.

D shouts from downstairs that it's time for us to go to the hospital. When I hear him coming up the stairs, I quickly snap the laptop shut. He is convinced that all this is bad for my blood pressure. I've told him about Herman, and that he'll be taking over for me, which is partly true.

"You coming?" D is in the hallway, holding my coat. We look at each other briefly, then he averts his eyes, smiling nervously. I know what he's thinking. I'm thinking it, too, I think it every time we drive to the hospital: this might be the last time we leave home without a baby. In the car, we fill the nervous silence with small talk. At the hospital entrance, we're so giddy that we get the giggles when an elderly man's slo-mo shuffling brings the revolving door to a halt.

At the obstetrics unit, Dr. Dukhi places a soft hand on my shoulder. "You're doing well, you've come really far, but now we're going to have to prepare for a different route than you'd hoped for." For a moment I think he's talking about Bommenneef, that Dr. Dukhi has been peering over my shoulder all this time and has come to the conclusion that I've definitely lost my way. "Let's try to stretch it another three weeks."

"Three?" I stare dumbfounded from Dukhi to D, whose blood has drained from his face. "But don't I still have eight weeks?" Dr. Dukhi shakes his head. "I'm afraid not. I don't want to take any risks." He removes his hand from my shoulder. "I realize you have to regroup, but don't worry about it too much. Everything will be fine."

I want to say that I'm not so sure, that I've just started my pregnancy class, that we haven't gotten any further than the labor dance and I have no idea what I have to do when the time comes. That I've still got deadlines and have a closet to clear out, and most importantly my son has to be given the right name, and to do that I have to have the right story, and since the story I had turns out to be inaccurate I have to at least come up with a good ending—all's well that ends well—but at the moment I'm stuck in a cul-de-sac of unanswered emails and Facebook messages and I haven't put anything right or even gotten my head around things, there are only questions that lead to more questions, I don't even know anymore if this is about courage and justice, who knows, maybe now it's about chaos and regret. I want to tell him that yesterday I took Bommenneef's citation—the yellowed proof of his heroism—off the wall, and that the wall looked so empty and meaningless that I hung the thing back up, and then took it down again and then hung it back up, and so on and so forth for another fifteen minutes. I want to say that three weeks isn't nearly enough, that I'm not ready, that I don't know what to tell my son about life, that I'll do everything wrong, that this is proof that I'm already a dud of a mother, not able to carry her child full term. But if I open my mouth now, I'll cry, so I nod at Dukhi and Dukhi nods back, and for a moment, just a brief moment, I am reassured.

At home I'm sent off to bed, cared for, lectured, cooed to sleep as if I'm the baby. My parents drop by, sisters and friends bring good soup and bad magazines. They urge me not to think of anything else, just let my mind go blank. The baby wriggles under my skin; its jutting limbs form weird bumps on my belly.

D lays down next to me as soon as he can, his head down near my abdomen, where he seems to be talking more to the baby than to me. Of course we're ready, he says, and pointing to the empty spot in between us on the bed he says he can't wait until our baby is lying there. "It can't be that difficult, hon, the whole world does it." I run my hands through his thick hair and would give anything in the world to change places with him.

3 WEEKS LEFT

I AM DISORIENTED BY the gap in our countdown. I keep opening my digital datebook. The full-year overview, then the separate months, days, the individual hours, as though I might unearth those five lost weeks among the white pixels in between the time divisions. I'm tempted to phone someone up—Dr. Dukhi, Kant, God—and demand the return of the missing weeks. But the only thing responsible for this leap in time is my own body, which does not measure time in weeks but in the velocity of my blood.

This morning, after yet another sleepless night, I was prepared to let it go. I'd drop the search and just wing it when the baby arrived. No more googling, phoning, emailing, speculating, slogging through dossiers and books. In my mind I folded up the map of Antarctica. Mission not accomplished. It gave me a vague sensation of liberation. But fifteen minutes later, Herman emailed. He had found the name of the family where one of Jacoba's sisters had been taken on as an au pair in 1946.

"It was a heck of a search, but I found the phone number of the girl she babysat. Who knows, maybe she kept contact with the sister."

I tap in the number, and they answer after a single ring. I'm startled by the old voice on the line. I had foolishly expected a small child, but the little girl of then is now probably in her late seventies.

I tell her the reason for my call.

"You're a year too late," the woman says. "Greetje died last year."

"Greetje?"

"The sister."

Greetje, the same as François's wife. It's starting to become a confusing name game: pretty much every name has an echo on the opposite side of the story.

"Do you think she would have wanted to talk to me, a relative of her sister's killer?"

"Maybe. And then, maybe not."

"Did she ever talk about the bomb?"

"No, but she did talk about Jackie."

"Who's Jackie?"

"Jacoba. But Jackie suits her better, or at least the Jacoba I knew."

I want to say that she couldn't possibly have known Jacoba,

but she corrects herself: "Not really *knew*, of course, but—how should I say it?—she had the starring role in my childhood stories. I was an only child and my parents were often out of the house, so Greetje and I were together every day. She talked a lot about her sister. They had grown up together in an orphanage in The Hague. Greetje told me how during the war, Jackie used to show up with food with the story that their dead mother had put it out for them. Greetje believed her, until the day Jackie got a beating because she'd been caught raiding the larder. She told me about Jackie's soft hair, and what they used to sing together in bed whenever one of them cried at night because they missed their mother so much. In Greetje's stories Jackie was a brave, beautiful girl; a combination of Cinderella and the Good Fairy. I used to beg her for more stories. Greetje had a vivid fantasy and thought up the funniest things: Jackie and the toothless apple, Jackie and the hundred frogs, Jackie and the meat-eating woods." The woman—the girl—laughs. "In fact, it was always the same story, just told differently. The world was threatened by a big bad something, and Jackie saved the day."

I asked if the bombing ever figured in the stories.

"No. I knew Jackie was dead, but it didn't mean much to me until one day—maybe it's not so nice to tell you this—well, there was a Van Heemstra Lane where we lived. It ran through the woods. A dark, windy path between the old trees. One day Greetje and I were walking there, and she saw the street sign and froze. I thought she was joking around, but she was really frozen stiff. When I pulled her arm, she didn't budge. She'd gone white as a sheet and her forehead was sweating. It lasted, oh, about twenty seconds, she didn't move a muscle, she just stood there looking at the name on that sign."

I hold my breath, hoping she'll say something about the attack, new facts that Greetje might have shared with her.

"When Greetje snapped out of it, she bent over and picked up a pinecone and hurled it at the street sign. On the way home she cried and told me how terribly she missed her sister. She said it was as if she'd lost an arm or a leg. And after that she said, 'If it were only my leg.'"

The woman pauses. Now it's my turn to say something, to react to this story, but my throat is clamped shut, my voice falters: the hormones, the fatigue, Jackie in the meat-eating woods. I think of Mrs. Koopmans's missing thumb. The stump in her rubber glove. A thumb for a life. I can't think of anything else to say but a raspy "Thank you."

"If you'd called a year earlier . . ."

"I know, I'm too late."

"It's okay."

"Well, goodbye, then."

I text Herman, thank him for the number, and let him know Greetje is no longer alive.

Soon after I push send, he calls. "I've got something better. The Bos family in Maassluis."

"The family who?"

"Bos. Jacoba's eldest sister."

After the story of Greetje and her storytelling, I am reluctant to call the Bos family out of the blue. Who knows what kind of Jacoba stories they grew up with, what kind of wounds I might reopen. I decide to send them an email, and I weigh my words carefully, keep it as neutral as possible. In the end the message consists of two dry sentences in which I introduce myself as Frans's niece who is trying to piece together the complete story of the Sinterklaas bombing.

———————

Two days later I'm sitting in a living room in Maassluis, way down on the other side of South Holland. Across from me are Jacoba's eldest sister, Annie's, five children. They are seated in a tight semicircle: two sisters and a brother on the sofa, another brother and sister in chairs on either side. I am installed in a large green armchair opposite them; in between us is a coffee table with an assortment of cocktail nibbles.

It's warm for this time of year, I'm overdressed and sweating. Even though I took plenty of time getting on the train— breathe calmly, no stress—and got a lift from the station, I'm exhausted now.

A mood of anxious expectation is hanging in the air. Cautiously smiling at these five faces across from me, it's the first time I sense I'm looking the story straight in the eye, that here in this living room, history is breathing and armed with questions. Something has been opened up: time, maybe.

The conversation gets rolling without difficulty. I tell them what I know, the siblings take turns sharing memories of Jacoba. They are secondhand memories, passed on by their mother and aunts. They call her Coby, not Jackie. And even though it's the same girl, the name Coby brings to mind someone different: an older, more sober person. They tell me that when their grandmother died, their grandfather remarried and placed seven of the ten children in an orphanage. Jacoba, still a baby, was raised by the nuns of the House of Mercy in The

Hague. The regime was depressing and decidedly unmerciful; the children mostly sought succor from one another. The nuns forced the younger orphans to eat their own vomit if they were sick. If you raised your voice, you'd be shut in a dark cupboard. Jacoba lived there until she was sixteen, at which time she was placed in a family as a housemaid. After two years' service she would be allowed to leave. She almost made it: in December 1946 she only had a few more months to go until, at last, her life could begin.

"But she wasn't badly off at the Boers'," the eldest brother says. His mother, Annie, had told them later, much later, how pleased she had been that Jacoba had found work there. Decent people who treated her well. The fact that she was there that Sinterklaas Eve showed she was part of the family.

One of the sisters, Coby, is named after Jacoba. Her grandfather spoiled her with gifts and attention, as though to make up for what his own daughter had been denied. I almost blurt out my intention of naming my son after my great-uncle, but I catch myself, afraid of causing offense. Coby was the one who heard the most about her deceased aunt. Her mother told her about sitting at Jacoba's deathbed, how long it all took, and how upset she was at the terrible injuries she had suffered. "The older she got, the more our mother talked about her," Coby says. "She said that the longer ago it was, the closer it felt."

They never heard anything about the perpetrators. The family probably just wanted to move on, says the eldest brother. "The war was over. There was no discussion about who was right and who was wrong. Too painful, maybe. And they had other things on their mind." But, he adds, "moving on" did not really work either. "There's still a hole, a wound. Part of the family had been amputated."

Occasionally the siblings get choked up, and then one has to take over from the other. But it's just a cracked voice or watery eyes—nobody really cries, it's secondhand grief, inherited from the previous generation. It gets passed around like a bowl of cocktail nuts, it gets stuck in my throat and I swallow it back.

I ask them to describe Jacoba's looks. The youngest brother leaves the room, returns with three photographs, and places them on the table. "I'll scan them and email them to you."

The largest one is a portrait. A serious girl with a pretty, full mouth and small, round glasses. The second one is of Jacoba and her sister Greetje, the sister that had made her into a fairy, a hero, a princess. They smile at the camera, their heads cocked close together. The last photo is blurry and taken from a distance. In it, a girl sits on a chair, alone, in a large, spartan dormitory. She does not look at the camera, her gaze is aimed downward at her small, bare feet. Her dress hangs crookedly and the bow in her hair looks rumpled. Everything about this picture exudes loneliness.

I look at the circle of siblings, at the bowls of nuts, and the photos of Jacoba. She might still be here if that bomb hadn't gone off. I want to say something, put things right, make amends. But everything that comes to mind sounds trite compared to that desolate dormitory where Jacoba counted the days until her life could begin.

"Say Frans was still alive. Is there anything you'd want to hear from him?" I ask. They hesitate. "What do you think could bring this story to a satisfactory conclusion?"

"Regret," says the youngest brother. "I would like to hear

him say he regrets it. That would be the only satisfactory ending."

That evening I lie, fat and dopey, in the semidarkness of my bedroom, looking at the blood specks on the palm tree wallpaper. I almost told them this afternoon that on his deathbed Frans said he was sorry. I felt I had to offer them something in the way of recompense, to give the affair some kind of closure. I so wanted to set things right—for them, for myself, for my son, for that girl in the dormitory. But I couldn't lie, not about this. I have to know for sure. And there is only one person I can ask: the man who sat at Frans's side shortly before he died, at his most honest moment.

If Juan Carlos is still alive, then surely he'll remember. You never forget a person's last words.

THE AIRBNB LISTING is too good to be true. An old villa in Bommenneef's neighborhood. One last-ditch effort to tie up the loose ends: the very spot where Bommenneef himself ended. From my room I would look out onto the courtyard and at the window behind which he slept and died back in 1987.

At least that's what the neighbor says. He came around yesterday, curious about what I was doing here in low season. He has only vague memories of "the old captain," as Frans was known in these parts. He remembers Frans being rather a loner, and that the local children were afraid of him. "He would sit for hours in his wheelchair staring out into the courtyard." At what? Neighbor doesn't know. "We thought he saw ghosts." He laughed, pointed to the palm in the middle of the courtyard. "Maybe he was just looking at that—it was there then too."

I have named the tree Methuselah, after the biblical patriarch. Or actually after the Israeli date palm I'd read about in *National Geographic* back in 2005 that was named after Methuselah. The tree had been cultivated from two-thousand-year-old seeds they had found on Masada. "Could Jesus have sat under this Methuselah tree?" asked the block-letter photo caption. That's a tricky one. It depends whether the potential tree, the seed, is the same thing as the real tree that eventually grows. No, I conclude at first. But Jesus (the historical one) and the seed did exist at the same time, so if you look at it that way, then you come out with a yes. But then, who says this palm tree, which has grown out of that seed, is the same palm tree that would have sprouted back then? It makes me dizzy, just as I get dizzy from the notion that Bommenneef could have seen me sitting here at this window, or I him, were it not for those intervening years.

My cell phone vibrates. It's D. He calls every few hours. The first day he was furious; he screamed at me that only a lunatic would spend the last few days of her pregnancy alone in some deserted seaside village in a foreign country. I had to admit he was right. Only when the plane landed in Barcelona did it hit me what a dumb idea this was. Before I'd even gotten off the jetway I had looked up and saved all the Spanish emergency numbers and the addresses of two nearby hospitals. On the train to Vinaròs I dozed off, a sentence by Salinger banging around in my head: *Mothers are all slightly insane*, and with that same sentence I awoke when we reached the small, sunny station.

For three days I've been in a continuous state of mild panic, but I don't want D to be any more anxious than he already is, so I try to sound calm.

"I'll be home tomorrow."

"You should've told me."

"You wouldn't have let me go."

"That's right. I'm coming down."

"I'll be gone before you get here."

By now he has resigned himself to it, mostly, I suspect, for the sake of the baby. Don't add to the stress. He checks in a few times a day, to make sure I'm still alive, that *we're* still alive.

"And?" he asks. "Found out anything new about the Lord of the Ring?"

I tell him I'll be meeting Juan Carlos this afternoon. I gave myself three days to locate him, which must be enough in a small town like Vinaròs. But it turns out Juan Carlos has moved. And it was no easy job to find someone who had his phone number. His English is poor, so the neighbor (who I think takes pity on me, a woman on her own and with such a bloated belly) interpreted for us. "The captain's niece is here and she'd like to talk to you." Juan Carlos is wary, perhaps he's afraid I suspect him of something. Nothing easier, of course, than to take a quick spin through the house of a dying man, let a wristwatch glide into your pocket. Via the neighbor I assure Juan Carlos that all I want is to find out about Frans's final hours. What the captain said before he died. The old grocer agrees to take the bus from the village where he now lives, an hour away.

D listens patiently to my progress report.

"This morning I kind of enjoyed being on my own," he says.

"A few days of calm before the storm. So I can finally let it sink in what we've gotten ourselves into." He painted the nursery, assembled a cupboard. He says he's scared stiff, but in a good way. I'm here, he assures me, and I'll always be. I say he's the only person in the world I'd want to do this with. Funny how distance creates closeness.

These days, the baby is more awake than ever. Maybe he feels that it's almost time. Four days ago Dr. Dukhi said that he's big enough to be delivered without too many complications.

After D hangs up, I lie down and close my eyes, just for a moment. Two hours later I bolt awake. The sun shines blindingly into every room—a surplus of sunlight, and nowhere a shadow. I check my phone. My appointment with Juan Carlos is in half an hour. I struggle out of bed. My ankles have started to swell up; pretty soon they, too, will be swallowed up by the fluid that my body has been collecting. I see in the bathroom mirror that my chin has started to vanish, and that the excess water has now settled in my wrists. My fingers tingle, my hands feel heavy and weak: it's the carpal tunnel syndrome the obstetrician warned about. Nothing to be done. There's nothing to be done about anything, except just have the baby.

Someone bangs on the door. The neighbor, holding his telephone. "It's Juan Carlos," he says. "He is sick." He asks if we can't just talk by phone. I look at the black iPhone. "Is he on the line?" The neighbor nods and switches to speaker mode.

"¡Hola!" An elderly, tinny voice.

"I'll translate for you," the neighbor says.

I gulp back my disappointment. I had pictured it otherwise. Juan Carlos and me on an idyllic Spanish terrace, where

Bommenneef's deepest thoughts would be revealed to me. His guilt, his regret, the residue of his life: the coda of a new, satisfactory story. But I don't have time to be critical. My plane leaves tomorrow. I have to get back to D; I have to have a baby.

I nod at the neighbor.

"Ask him about Frans's final hours. What he said before he died. How he left life behind."

I listen anxiously as the neighbor translates the questions. We stand bent over the iPhone, the portal through which the oracle gives its answers in crackly, elderly Spanish.

"Juan Carlos says he mostly swore," says the neighbor. "He was angry about dying. They drank together, drank a lot. The captain said that the envelope on his desk still needed to be mailed." That must have been the ring. "He said I could have the sardines in the fridge," Juan Carlos continues, "and that he wanted to be buried without socks. We had a good laugh about that, because of his legs. He asked if I would sprinkle him with perfume after he died. He didn't smell so nice—like mushrooms and manchego—because he refused to be washed those last weeks."

I interrupt. "Tell him he can skip the details. I want to know about the real things, the big things."

The neighbor gives me a surprised look, and translates. Juan Carlos hesitates, asks something. "What do you mean by 'big' things?" says the neighbor.

"If he had any regrets," I sigh. "I want to know if he was sorry about anything from the past, something he might want to get off his chest, apologize for, make good."

The neighbor repeats this to Juan Carlos.

The tinny voice falls silent. "He asked me to put his wheelchair out on the street," he says. "He thought someone might come along that needed it. The thing sat there on the sidewalk for a month, then I brought it to the garbage. It was rusted through."

The neighbor asks something with *más*. I know that word, *más*: "more." Whether there was anything more.

"No," says the oracle. "Nada más."

Twilight on the beach. A chill wafts in from the sea. I shiver. I should have brought my jacket, but it's back in the apartment, packed in my suitcase. No need to worry about Bommenneef; he's tucked snugly in his wheelchair, a warm rug draped over the stumps of his legs. He breathes heavily; every now and then he lets out a soggy smoker's hack and spits into the sand. I had expected to find him sitting at the window, where the children used to see him looking for ghosts, but he was on the beach, facing the sea, the wheels of his chair sunk into the coarse sand. As though someone brought him here long ago, and then forgot him.

When I sat down next to him, he looked up briefly and then stared back out into space.

His face is fuller than I had expected, fat and gray like an elephant's.

"So here you are," I say.

For one perfect moment, we sit silently next to each other amid the sound of the waves and the traffic on the boulevard behind us. But there's no time to lose. Once the sun has set it'll only get colder, and my plane is leaving in a couple of hours.

Where should I start? At the most important part. "You have to tell me something honest. End things with the truth."

He looks at me, his eyes are deep and watery, a hint of a smile on his mouth.

"I've disproved lies," I continue, "but I've lied too. I named your best friend 'B,' even though her name doesn't start with a B. I've fudged the chronology of my search because it works better not to discover everything at once. I've ascribed my questions and answers to others; I've pretended you were given speeding tickets in the 1930s when I don't even know for sure if there was such a thing as speed limits back then, but it looked good for the character sketch; I said we ate cocktail nuts at Jacoba's family's house in Maassluis when we really ate pie, but I needed an image to go with the grief that got passed around the circle. You only pass a slice of pie once, and you don't share it, that's why I changed it to nuts, and there are so many more things, too many to name. But most of all I've kept things to myself, which is the worst form of lying. I've kept to myself that you were involved in that horrible abduction of an innkeeper in Renkum who your gang was planning to crucify, I mean really crucify, to let him bleed to death, with a wooden sign above his head that said 'This Is How Holland Rebuilds.' I kept quiet about an item in the *Utrechts Dagblad* that said you put your army superiors Goedewagen and Drost on your hit list because of a conflict about your smuggling activities—in this light the bombing, too, looks more like a payback than some ethical, righteous deed. Nowhere did I mention that several articles refer to you as 'St. Nicholas of Death.' I've covered for you, because I wasn't prepared to just give up the myth. You were a dangerous man, a lunatic murderer, but for twenty-five years you were also my hero. You don't erase something like that so easily. I wanted to peel the myth down to its core, but a myth is an onion and has no core. And yet I don't want to end up with nothing, I need a name and a story, so I invented new, better layers. But this isn't something I can turn into fiction: you killed people, real people, ruined real lives, and I need something as real as Jacoba's ruined eye.

"That's why we're sitting here on this deserted beach, you and I, and that's why I'm giving you the last word. I don't care what you say, as long as it's honest. No, that's not true either. I already know what your last words should be. And if you don't say them yourself, I'll put the words in your mouth. 'I'm sorry.' Go on, say it. And make it sound like you mean it."

The old man stares stoically into space.

I wait. I wait until I can't wait anymore. Then I go. I turn a few times as I walk up to the boulevard, but the man does not look back.

———

D picks me up from the airport. The house smells like fresh paint and laundry detergent. It's quiet in the rooms, like somebody holding their breath. The cradle is standing in the middle of my office. Its side panels—dark red before I left—are now ice blue.

There's an oblong case on the windowsill with a pink ribbon around it.

"For you," D says. He points at my belly. "For us."

It's a small telescope.

D laughs and gestures around the blue-and-white room. "If

we ever want to make this into a planetarium, we've got to start somewhere."

I inspect the lenses and the ocular and get choked up at the idea that soon I'll have a son who one day will look at the stars, who will wonder how far away the planets are, and where light comes from, and all that darkness.

1 WEEK LEFT

IT'S GOING TO be a Christmas baby. The date is fixed, even what time they'll hook me up to the labor-inducing IV. "It's time to deliver," Dr. Dukhi said during our last visit. What a strange way of putting it: "deliver." Like a package.

It's so strange to know exactly when he'll come, attaching a date to the unimaginable.

I send the photos to Herman with the note: "For your web." The next day, he emails back.

A friend of mine is an archeologist. He spent forty years digging in a mound in Syria, peeled back a thousand years of history, and sorted it into boxes. I asked him once what the best thing was that he found in all those years. He answered: sometimes a skeleton is more than an archeological find. Suddenly the outline of a person fills out the space around the bones. And that's what you do it for. For the moment that you can say to a skull: "I'll rescue you from the past, I'll bring you back from limbo. Even though you've been lying under this rubble for a thousand years now and everyone has forgotten your name, I will give you a human face." Cheers, H.

3 DAYS LEFT

I TRY TO RECONSTRUCT how you got here, in this plastic wheeled crib. There was a start—they put in a balloon catheter ("we're going to inflate a balloon in your cervix"—this sounds more festive than it was) to induce labor.

Then there was half a day and a full night in which we anxiously waited for the water.

And then it broke.

I remember a mishmash of images, sounds, and smells. There was screaming—from me, from the gynecologist, from your father, from women in other rooms—screaming everywhere and an awful internal cracking, as though bones had to make way for your head. There was dimmed lighting that made me feel as though I was in a kind of limbo, a ghoulish world into which we could vanish at any moment. I wanted the lights on full blast, to see and be seen, but every time I started to ask, a new contraction wrenched me and I heard myself growl and roar, a deep, raw, caked-on sound, and through all the contractions I was ashamed of that roaring—*this isn't me,* I cried, *this isn't me*—but I kept getting drowned out by an old and angry woman in my throat, someone said *just one more push and you're there*, and they kept repeating and repeating it, until I knew for sure I couldn't anymore. I remember being emptied, like a blown-out egg, you were dangling above me, dark purple, covered from head to toe with a slimy film, and the first thing that came to mind was the overripe plum I once found at the bottom of my backpack, months after I'd put it in there and forgotten about it. I remember your father's astonished face and a sudden burst of laughter—from him? from me?—because of the absurdity of it all, this purple *thing*, this prehistoric plum that was supposed to be the symbol of our love. And then four rubber gloves lifting you above my belly, up toward my breast, I look at your head, an attempt at recognition, at feeling something as this primeval pate comes at me, crinkled and angry, a bloody glob, more wrinkle than skin. All nineteen inches of you lands with a sucking noise on my breastbone, and the only thing I can think is: Who is this? And then, immediately, the answer: this is me.

My parents come in, and when my mother sees me, she bursts into tears—there's something wrong with me, I can see it on her face. The pediatrician comes in next, inspects your little insect-legs, your skull, she runs her fingers along your back, and then nods. You get a score. Something with a seven, I think out of ten. Not bad, but not good either. Too low for what has just happened. The pediatrician looks at me, and for a fraction of a second I see her grimace.

How terrible do I look?

For now we'll have to stay in the hospital for observation, she says. My blood pressure is still too high. She talks some more, I see her mouth move but nothing sinks in, I only hear you cry, the pediatrician's head dissolves into blotches, then gels back together, someone comes in to say stitches are required, someone else says something about a vacation on Tenerife, and someone says that a child leaves behind an internal wound that takes a long time to heal.

Child, wound—those words echo inside my head, which is now entirely empty, the words ricochet off the walls, bounce against my skull. *A child, a wound.*

"What's his name?" someone asks. And I almost say the name I gave you fifteen years ago. Back when you were just a fantasy, a prospect. Back when I still believed my heroes were heroes, and the story could be passed on without objection.

"I don't know," I mumble. A chubby nurse wheels us down to the farthest room on the ward.

In the parking lot under my window, among the cars, is a decorated Christmas tree. Its tiny lights flicker in the wet snow. Families walk down the corridor of my ward carrying oversized balloons and platters full of food. The smell of chicken and garlic mingles with the chemical odor of a hospital room and a strange, sweet stench that reminds me of a zoo. The reptile habitat, or no, the monkeys. The visitors in the corridor whisper so as not to wake the babies, but their wet shoes make a loud, sucking noise on the floor, like a herd of heavy animals in a swamp.

Behind every blue door on the long, white corridor is a new mother. Like storks, big and weak on their white beds. Next to them, a plastic nest on wheels with the egg they just laid.

Your crib is higher than my bed, and I see only the top of your blue-and-pink hospital cap. You whimper. A midwife tells me you're feeling queasy, and probably will be for some time yet. Of all the sensations being born might elicit, queasiness is probably the last one I'd think of. It sounds like a minor, temporary inconvenience. The result of a bad mussel or a hangover, not the violence of the past twenty-four hours, in which we have been torn from a single creature into two.

Outdoors, the streetlamps jump on, and for a moment I consider flipping on the bedside lamp, too, but it feels like an intrusion. I'm pleased with the early darkness and our dim togetherness. I don't quite dare look at you in full light yet.

Your father is out in the corridor, on the phone.

He reports your weight, your length. "No," I hear him say, "that hasn't been settled yet."

The door slides open. It's the nurse. She wants to know if we've made up our minds. I shake my head.

She nods patiently. But the system is not as patient as she is.

A person has to be mapped, defined, and encapsulated in a name within three days.

She takes a pen from her breast pocket and writes "Baby" on a form. Baby—this is how the system will recognize you for the time being, a generic designation, capitalized to make it look more like a name. I look at your bald head with its remaining splotches of blood and amniotic fluid, the name Baby doesn't suit something that looks like something that has been around for centuries. "We've got two days," the nurse says, "to change Baby into a proper name." She takes my blood pressure and nods, satisfied. "Getting there."

ACCORDING TO THE clock, six hours have passed, but where they've gone, I haven't the foggiest. Have I slept? You're lying on my chest, groaning: Did I take you out of your crib? I don't dare move. Why isn't there anyone in here with us? They've left me in here with this exotic animal that will die soon without professional care. It's irresponsible, leaving you and me alone in this room. Somebody with the proper diplomas should come who can make you stop groaning. I reach out to press the red button, call for help, but something happens with you, you squeak and whimper and then shift, or squirm— something in between slink and crawl, like a worm or a mole— upward over my belly, your eyes are shut, you explore my skin with pursed lips, inch by inch upward toward my breast. I don't help you, I don't call out to you, I just lie there motionless and watch this subterrestrial wriggling. I don't know where you get the strength or your sense of direction, but you make a beeline for my breast, claw your fingers into my flesh, grope for a grip and find it, clamp your toothless mouth onto my nipple, and, with amazing strength, start sucking.

A name—I have to get moving on your name, but I dissolve into a white mist, I lie stock-still in bed with a purple worm attached to my breast, a bloody mole, a human-fleshed fish.

It is seven o'clock—a.m. or p.m., I have no idea—and there's furious screaming coming from the corridor, another birth. I'm reminded of the rhino baby that I watched being born in the zoo in Rotterdam. It's what the dinosaurs must have sounded like, the habitat's attendant said. In the next room a baby howls nonstop. Rubber soles squeak hurriedly along the linoleum floor, rain slams against the windows.

Our door opens, it's D with the nurse in tow. D gingerly lifts you off the bed, cradles you in his arms, kisses you, kisses me. The nurse checks my blood pressure. It's gone down some more. She says I can take a shower. "The chance that you'll faint now is pretty slim," she says.

D rocks you in his arms. It looks so natural, you and he, that motion.

The nurse sets a chair in front of me.

"Lean on this."

I try to lift myself up, but cringe with pain. It's like someone has put a knife between my legs that digs deeper into me with every move.

"I can't do it."

She goes out into the hallway and comes back with a stack of three more chairs, and lines them up leading to the bathroom.

"Go on, walk, lean on them."

I drag myself from one chair to the next, and with each movement the knife makes me gasp for air. There's a fourth chair in the shower stall, but I don't want to take a shower, I don't want to move anymore; I've dragged myself here so that I can look in the mirror. I want to see what alarmed the pediatrician, why my mother burst into tears.

The mirror is to the left of the door. A small, square thing. I glance at it, and my first reaction is that it's a small window and on the other side is a huge, crazed woman. It's the classic horror scene: woman looks in mirror and sees a deranged version of herself. My face is so swollen that my nose and mouth are almost entirely sucked into it, a hideous hunk of flesh with two red holes: my bloodshot eyes. My shiny skin is a landscape of burst veins branching out across my face. My neck and shoulders are riddled with small pink pimples, like a subdermal rash, my lips are peeling and dehydrated. Only my hair, my hair is more beautiful than it's ever been: it hangs full and glossy in thick brown waves over my shoulders.

Half in shock, I shuffle over to the shower. Why not? I sink into the chair, let tepid water run over my body. Again that cloying animal smell. It's me. The smell of the monkey cage wafts up from between my legs, it's the wound, a sweetish, sickening combination of blood and amniotic fluid.

A child, a wound.

I want to stay here forever, never go outside, I've done what I was supposed to do, I've brought a new person into the world, and now I just want to disappear—no, I've already disappeared, sacrificed myself for the baby. I am not this wreck that's been left behind.

D calls my name. The nurse knocks at the door.

They help me back out, dress me in clean clothes, tell me I look better than yesterday. Jesus. I cry. The nurse strokes my hair.

"You'll see how fast it goes. Pretty soon you'll have forgotten all this, and all you'll be is happy with your handsome little man."

"Two handsome little men." D smiles his Mentos smile and for a moment, a very brief moment, the pain is gone.

D helps me into a wheelchair and places you on my lap. We roll out into the corridor.

"Family outing," he says jovially. "Get our baby a nice clean diaper."

Our baby. It sounds good, but I know it's not true. You're mine, you're me. There are two more storks at the communal changing table, their oversized pajamas hang over their puffy, empty bellies. We smile at one another, we whisper vowel sounds at our babies—ooh, aah—it all just happens, this collective cooing, without me really being aware of it.

When they ask your name, I give them your temporary one. Baby. They're taken aback. "That's too bad," says the stork with the biggest pajamas.

D laughs. "We'll have a name tomorrow."

We sleep. You drink. D and I eat lasagna; it's the best lasagna we've ever eaten. When we ask a nurse to give our compliments to the kitchen, she chuckles. "The recipe is tomato sauce, a week in the freezer, and childbirth."

1 DAY LEFT

I ASK D TO bring a mirror from home so I don't need to keep staggering to the bathroom to see if I've started looking like myself again.

When he gets back, he sets Bommenneef's ring on the nightstand. "I thought you might want to wear it again."

I hesitate, look at my hands, which in two days have shrunk to almost their normal size. Then I slide it onto my middle finger. The gold feels cool against my skin.

Family comes to visit, they bring you clothes and a set of dishes. You get picked up; the first time, it feels like I'm the one sailing through the air and lying against the torso of a grandma or grandpa, but the distance grows by the hour, as though the process of being born keeps on going, and, slowly but surely, you slip ever farther out of me. I miss you.

Everyone asks for your name.

That evening the ward is quiet for the first time. No births, only the voice of Mariah Carey coming from a distant radio. You lie on my stomach and make strange, high-pitched sounds. I reply in kind, a fish-to-fish sonar conversation, one of us is breathing heavily. There is a heart beating fast and furiously. Yours? Mine? Ours.

My blood pressure is stable and has dropped sufficiently. We can go home tomorrow. I had wanted to say we are not ready, that we're not prepared for this new situation, this being two people. I wanted to ask if they'd put you back in, so I could walk around forever with a fat belly and only the prospect of new personhood, rather than this huge, open life we now face.

I think of Frans and Carolina, of the baby who was sucked into the cosmos after just one day, and I'm so sorry that you have to become someone, *are* someone, that I can no longer protect you from life, or protect myself. I want snow. I want a white, muffled world, but it's raining and storming outside, things shake, make noise, glisten with wetness. I'm sorry that one day I will disappoint you, and you me, that soon I'll no longer feel your heart beating in my own chest, that already you're drifting away from me, that D and I will saddle you with photos, stories, myths, and expectations, with families, and with deep, undefined fears that plague our reptilian brain. I'm sorry that one day you'll come home and ask why there's war, and who's good and who's bad—and this is if all goes well, if you yourself don't get caught up in the violence we now fear. I'm so sorry that one day you might have to make the decision I never had to make (at least not yet), to go with the flow or to resist, I'm sorry that you'll learn that no one gets to the finish line with entirely clean hands, that this is a world where we tend to downplay what's good because we know too much and don't dare hope enough.

You were born looking upward: just as I went into labor you did a half twist, they call it a "stargazer," and I think of those wooden gears in that attic in Franeker, that small, overwhelming backroom universe, the Kant quote, the moral law in me and in the starry sky above me.

The stars.

I wake D up, who is sleeping on a cot next to our bed.

"I've made up my mind."

He lays a drowsy hand on mine.

"Good," he mumbles, "that's good," and slips back to sleep.

THE DAY

D PACKS OUR BAGS while you lie asleep on my belly. When I studied my face in the mirror just now, for the hundredth time, I recognized a tiny hint of myself. D goes down to the cafeteria to get us breakfast.

A nurse walks in. "Let's wash the baby so he'll be nice and clean to go home."

She gently wipes your head with a washcloth, the last bits of blood, the last traces of my insides. The skin underneath is lighter than I had expected, several tints lighter than mine: your father's color.

She rinses the washcloth in the bathroom and comes back to do your hands. She points out your long nails.

"Maybe you should bite some off, otherwise he's liable to scratch himself."

"Bite?"

She nods. "They're too small for a nail clipper, so for now, biting is best."

She lifts you up, holds you with your fingers up near my mouth, and nods encouragingly.

I take your tiny thumb, cautiously put the hard ridge of the nail between my teeth, and bite. The nail gives; there's a sharp sliver on my tongue, and, surprised, I swallow it. Finger by finger I nibble off the edges and make your fingers soft and safe, until the nurse approvingly inspects your hands.

"He's ready."

I don't ask what for. Being cuddled. Shaking hands. A date. Love.

D is back. "Everything's packed. The kitchen's stocked, there's a blanket on the sofa . . . anything I've forgotten?"

The nurse carefully puts the hospital cap on your head and informs us that Dr. Dukhi will be along any minute for one last check. Then we can go.

"When we get home," I say to D, "can you go upstairs and take down that certificate?"

D nods. "I'll go get the car," he says before disappearing into the corridor.

The nurse lays you back on my lap. "I wish you all the best." She walks to the door. I press you against me, feel how warm and firm you are, feel how fast your heart beats, faster than mine. I kiss your clean head. Here we go.

I kiss you again and clear my throat.

"He has a name."

My voice sounds strange. Low and husky.

The nurse turns, her hand on the doorknob.

"Sorry?"

"He has a name," I repeat. Louder this time.

"Just in time," she laughs. "I'll go get a pen and paper."

Acknowledgments

This book could not have been written without all the fantastic people who provided me with information, and who may or may not recognize themselves in the story I have created from the story.

I am extremely grateful to Maarten Biermans for having bought the box of Frans's documents, and to Sonia Eijkman for sorting the contents and bringing me the box. Many thanks to the van Santen family, who provided me with information about Elize; to Sylvia de Vlaming, who put me in touch with the van Santens; and to the mysterious Mr. Madarasz, who steered me onto several right tracks. The hours spent with Mrs. Rijshouwer-van Wely and Mrs. Gatsonides were invaluable, as was the extensive *Geschiedenis van de Binnenlandse Veiligheids-dienst* by Dick Engelen, which perhaps is not the ideal book to read when you're dog-tired and pregnant, but under any other circumstances is highly recommended reading.

My thanks to the Bos family for information regarding their Jacoba, to Hajo Wildschut for the gynecological feedback, to Otto Nelissen's afternoon naps, which made it possible for me to get this book finished at all, and to my dear uncle Frans, for whom this ring was actually intended, but that's another story.

Deep respect for Liet Lenshoek, whom I could always bother with my questions and doubts, and bravo to Matin van Veldhui-zen for her keen eye and cheese sandwiches. Then a big kiss for the whole *Das Mag* team, and especially for the indispensable Marscha and Daniël.

The men and women at the National Archives were ex-tremely helpful, with my special thanks to Peter Wijnmaalen, who assured me that the entrance hall has changed in recent years, and that my recollection of it was more or less correct (as far as memories can be correct, that is—but enough about that). Except that the revolving door was a sliding door, Peter said. But the choice between revolving and sliding seems to me an easy one.

About the Author

The Dutch poet, novelist, and playwright Marjolijn van Heemstra holds a master's degree in religion. Her first poetry collection, *If Moses Had Been More Persistent*, won the Jo Peters Poetry Prize. She debuted as a novelist with *The Last of the Aedemas*. Her latest novel, *In Search of a Name*, was nominated for multiple national prizes and has been translated into nine languages. She currently writes for *The Correspondent, Harper's Bazaar*, and several newspapers.